'To my dear, sweet Grandmother, Miss Edna and my grandson Myles. You have both been such an inspiration. Thank you.'

One Mother's Pain

Short Stories for Night Owls

Darlene Torey

BALBOA.PRESS
A DIVISION OF HAY HOUSE

Front Cover Image by Laura Crewes.

Balboa Press books may be ordered through booksellers or by contacting:

Balboa Press
A Division of Hay House
1663 Liberty Drive
Bloomington, IN 47403
www.balboapress.co.uk
UK TFN: 0800 0148647 (Toll Free inside the UK)
UK Local: 02036 956325 (+44 20 3695 6325 from outside the UK)

Scriptures marked KJV are taken from the KING JAMES VERSION (KJV): KING JAMES VERSION, public domain.

Print information available on the last page.

ISBN: 978-1-9822-8214-1 (sc)
ISBN: 978-1-9822-8218-9 (hc)
ISBN: 978-1-9822-8217-2 (e)

Balboa Press rev. date: 09/22/2020

CONTENTS

Part 1

Part 2

PART 1

ONE MOTHER'S PAIN

Seeing the Mother, choked by sadness,
she's burying her daughter feeling like
she's the only one in the world. So I shed one tear.
—Calvin CKerr

CHAPTER 1

In January 1955, momentous times lay ahead for one young woman living in Jamaica, she was about to embark on a life-changing journey to Britain. Sitting under a large, shady almond tree, she calmly contemplated her future plans.

The Jamaican nation was also in expectant mood. Their hopes soared high when a young Jamaican solider, Norman Manley, was awarded the Military Medal for serving in the Royal Field Artillery during World War I. He was a brilliant scholar, athlete, and, lawyer. Driven by his political ambition, Manley founded and went on to lead the People's National Party (PNP) to a triumphant win in the general election earlier that month, becoming the chief minister of Jamaica. Did the mild earthquake which occurred on election day foreshadow events that would subsequently change the fortunes of both the PNP and the young woman? It would remain to be seen. The earthquake in no way dampened the spirit of the nation. Neither did it deter the process of decolonisation, which could now begin in earnest.

CHAPTER 2

Across the Atlantic, ten years after World War II, Britain was bankrupt. It would require an immense effort by the government to reboot the economy and rebuild the country's extensively damaged infrastructure. There was an urgent need to resolve labour shortages caused by the mobilisation of armed forces, the necessary expansion of the merchant navy, as well as the government's need to control industries that had been vital to the war effort, such as steel and agriculture. The country also faced a chronic shortfall of nurses. To address the crisis, Britain reached out to its commonwealth countries through collaborative recruitment campaigns.

An advertisement posted in a local newspaper in search of trainee nurses caught the attention of Miss Mae, a talented dressmaker living in Jamaica. Her curiosity was aroused. Not only was she a firm believer that a child's interest should be acknowledged and followed, she was aware that this might be a chance for her eldest daughter to make a fresh start and realise her childhood dream of becoming a qualified nurse. She learned from her enquiries that the British government had devised various schemes to assist with fares to Britain. She hastened to arrange for her daughter to attend a recruitment session. The young woman easily met the criteria, which required that candidates were aged between 18 to 30 years old, literate, and willing to sign a three-year contract. If she was accepted, she would undertake her nursing training in Britain.

The opportunity undoubtedly raised several issues for the young woman. She questioned her ability to cope with the training. How would she manage her reaction at the sight of an injured patient's blood? Would she be able to successfully administer patient's injections or dress their wounds adequately? Further, and most importantly, she had to consider the needs of her three young children. She knew only too well that the implications for the children included them remaining with her family in Jamaica for a minimum of three years, possibly even longer.

What really excited her most of all was the idea of being free, for the first time in her life, from Miss Mae's, jurisdiction, and that of George Horton, the father of her two youngest children, Delton and Denise. Her ties to Thadius Granger, the father of her eldest daughter, Jumokah, had been severed by him some four years earlier.

Miss Mae was the matriarchal head of her household. Her family had resided in Connor Town, since her childhood. Her father, a building contractor, originally from the suburban parish of St James in the county of Cornwall, had built two adjoining houses on Bloomberg Street. The larger of the two properties was sold at the time of his death. She had continued living in the remaining property with her husband, Papa Gustavia, their five children, and her eldest sister, Rose-Anne.

As her travel plans progressed, the young woman was mindful of Miss Mae's input and her efforts to make the trip possible.

Being a nurse may be all she had ever dreamed of doing, but she was terrified of letting her mother down. Therefore, the prospect of living independently in Britain away from her family, was overshadowed somewhat by these and another growing concern which, for the time being, she chose to keep secret from her family. Miss Mae, on the other hand, saw beyond the possibilities that the training programme offered, she was determined to use it as a means of getting her daughter as far away as possible from the influence of George Horton.

CHAPTER 3

The entire family stood together in the front garden as the young woman waited by the gate in readiness to leave. She glanced fleetingly at a fragrant rose bush growing in the middle of the garden. She would later recall that it was ladened with delicate peach-coloured blossoms. Her children were unaware that she would not be returning for some time.

"Where yu a go Mummy? Can we come with yu?" they implored petulantly as they ran towards her.

She knew that their heart-rending plea would continue to haunt her long after she left the island. Embracing each of them in turn, she kissed them tenderly. But it was her youngest daughter, Denise, who moved her intensely. Her fragile health had always been a worry. She reluctantly released Denise from her arms before handing her over to her mother and her aunt Rose-Anne. Between them, they would care for her children. Turning away sharply, she climbed hurriedly into a waiting taxi which would to take her to Kingston Harbour. She waved through the window until it was unbearable for her to look at her children any longer.

"Please, let's go now," she urged the driver.

The car roared into life and sped away from the house. She

whispered doubtfully to herself, "I hope me a do the right thing?" before sinking back heavily into the car seat.

When the taxi drew to a halt at the harbour, she was met by Mr Horton. He was smartly attired in Oxford bag trousers, a crisp white shirt, and fashionable two-toned brogue shoes. His jacket was folded casually over one arm. He attracted the attention of a porter to collect her luggage. Holding open the door, he assisted her to step out onto the wharf. He cast his eyes up and down the length of her trim figure in unadulterated admiration. She was elegantly dressed in a lightweight tailored two-piece linen suit. The buttonless jacket she wore cut away on either side and rested slightly above her waistline, which concealed its own secret. Her mid-length skirt showed off her pretty little ankles and neat feet, which were attractively adorned in smart new black leather court shoes that pinched her toes mercilessly.

"You look stunning," he said quietly. She lowered her eyes self-consciously and fiddled with her tiny clutch bag containing her passport and other essential travel documents.

They walked slowly together towards the ship where a cacophony of noisy activity exuded from the great throng of passengers gathered on the wharf. Many of them carried large packages wrapped in brown paper and tied with string, in addition to baskets full of the familiar foods of home, fresh fruits, salt-fish fritters, fried fish and bammy, a traditional Jamaican flatbread made from cassava flour. Other necessities, packed tightly into large trunks, suitcases, and boxes, were stacked several feet high on the dock, alongside all the provisions needed for the 4,685-mile journey. The ship's crew worked steadily throughout the day, gradually transforming the landscape of the dock to reveal the port side of the *Asdania*. In due course, the huge mountain of cargo and luggage was consumed deep inside the hold of the ship.

Most of the travelling male passengers were proudly dressed in their best suits and ties. Their hats, set at rakish angles, gave them an aura of flamboyance and carefreeness. There was an unmistaken buzz of sanguinity in the air. A friendly camaraderie developed amongst them as they crowded together on the pier feverishly sharing their collective vision and ambitious thoughts of what they optimistically expected to accomplish in Britain. The women wore stylish suits and hats that were woefully inadequate for the inclement weather they would later encounter. Filled with self-importance, they flaunted their colourful handwoven straw baskets. A few of these women were lucky enough to travel with their children. Thousands of less fortunate children were left in Jamaica to be cared for by relatives. The emotional impact of the separation from their parents would affect their lives long into the future.

The time to board the *Asdania* was imminent. The young woman's forced air of self-confidence suddenly deserted her. She felt exposed and vulnerable. Hesitating at the foot of the gangplank, she attempted to collect herself. Glancing over her shoulder towards Mr Horton, she anxiously sought his reassurance.

"Please don't forget, I want to hear from you the minute you arrive," he insisted.

He continued watching her from across the pier until she set foot on the ship's deck. A pang of envy struck his heart as he observed passengers impatiently crowding past her onto the decks in an effort to catch final glimpses of their loved ones and friends. Mr Horton would not be accompanying the young woman on her journey. He would remain in Jamaica, having negated any other possible choice available to him. He was already married. Along with the two children he had fathered with the young woman, he also had three children with his wife.

CHAPTER 4

On deck, the young woman felt bewildered. She found it unnerving to be at the centre of such a large crowd. She was unaccustomed to the sound of so many people speaking at the same time. Pushing her way cautiously to the edge of the deck rail, she leaned across it tentatively. Her eyes misted over, and she felt a lump rising in her throat. She strained to catch a final glimpse of Mr Horton. Their eyes meet fleetingly before he turned and moved away. She continued gazing intently in his direction, willing him to turn around and come back. Instead, he disappeared from sight. She hesitated again, unsure what to do next.

Looking around her, the young woman secured a seat which overlooked the harbour. Taking in a deep breath of salty sea air, she relaxed her head against the back of the seat. Her eyelids felt heavy as a clear image of Thadius materialised in front of her. This striking, very dark-skinned young man, standing over six feet in height, had been very much in love with her. She had been attracted to his big personality and brilliant white teeth that parted easily into a luminous smile. He had been keen to marry. Unhappily for them, Miss Mae had adamantly refused to allow it to happen. She had no faith in their ability, at 17 and 18 years old respectively, to take on the challenge of marriage and assume responsibility for their newborn baby. Her decision would later have a detrimental effect on the lives of the couple.

A passenger's bag inadvertently brushed against the young woman's leg startling her from her thoughtful state of mind. An apology was duly proffered, which she readily accepted. Wrestling to make sense of her conflicted emotions, she sat alone long after family members, friends, and well-wishers had returned to their homes. In time, she stood up and leaned across the deck rail to observe final traces of the vibrant red and orange sun which faded mystically into the sea. The tropical dusk silently drew the day to a close, enveloping the harbour in a dark, navy, velvety cloak. The stars gradually appeared one by one, sparkling like tiny diamonds set against the backdrop of the evening sky. The *Asdania* slowly set sail, smoothly manoeuvring its way out of the harbour. The noise from the thick hub of passengers receded as they dispersed, retreating to their cabins below deck.

Looking out for the very last time across the Caribbean Sea, at the tiny island which had always been her home, the young woman fought to hold back the tears welling up in her eyes. Returning to her seat she continued to reflect on the events in her life that had culminated in her journey to Britain.

"Me can't turn back now," she murmured to herself.

CHAPTER 5

Her ill-fated association with Mr Horton now came vividly to mind. She had met him through his friendship with her brother, Martin. Women had always been a weak area for Mr Horton, and whenever he frequented Bloomberg Street, he found himself becoming irresistibly drawn to the young woman. As he got to know her better, he discovered that she was reserved and secretive by nature. He took advantage of these qualities, using them to gain her trust, before boldly proceeding to embark on a relationship with her in Thadius's absence. He intentionally concealed his true circumstances from her family.

Martin and Mr Horton had much in common. They were motivated by their personal interests. Martin, being a keen car mechanic since the age of fourteen, worked long hours at a nearby garage. In his spare time, nothing pleased him more than tinkering with old cars. His backyard was filled with spare parts. It was his sole ambition to build his own car one day. Mr Horton, on the other hand, had made short work of becoming one of the first welders in Connor Town to open his own welding business. This was no small achievement, given that welding was an emerging and highly skilled discipline. In next to no time, he was an accepted visitor at the young woman's home. He had also succeeded in making a good first impression with Miss Mae and Rose-Anne.

"My dear sister, what a pleasant boy. Yu know se him have him own welding shop. I like his ambition and energy." Miss Mae waxed lyrically to Rose-Anne as they prepared lunch together. "Such admirable qualities that are rarely to be found these days." She continued, "Mark my words, if he keeps up like this, that boy will go a long way." Rose-Anne agreed wholeheartedly with her sister, as she was generally inclined to do.

Miss Mae, who was fully engaged with her own demanding dressmaking business, paid little attention to neither her daughter nor to Martin and Mr Horton. The young men were often seen spending long hours together exchanging ideas and examining and re-examining all the spare parts Martin had carefully assembled at the back of the yard to build his car. Mr Horton carried out all the welding requirements for the project. They worked together with relentless enthusiasm for weeks. The results were truly inspired.

Much to the astonishment of scores of doubters they succeeded in building Fly Low, a tiny red two-seater car. What is more, Fly Low pulled off her first incredible maiden journey to Hanover flawlessly. The combination of two good-looking men in a car turned the heads of several pretty girls they met along the way. Much to their delight, some of them were fortunate enough to be taken for a spin. With their egos filled to the brim, it was an unforgettable and thrilling day. Fly Low was popular with everyone, and the car quickly became the talk of the town.

In the intervening period, the young woman's feelings for Mr Horton deepened. He shamelessly flirted with her, toying thoughtlessly with her fragile emotions. She, in keeping with her secretive nature, acted deviously. Very foolishly she facilitated his impromptu late-night visits. It was not long before she bore him two children. Miss Mae was irate with them both. She had naively presumed to rest her hope on Mr Horton's expected offer of marriage to her daughter, which so far had not been forthcoming.

Nevertheless, following the birth of their children, Mr Horton established a routine of visiting the young woman every Sunday to bring them food and money. However, quite unexpectedly, early one Saturday morning, he arrived at her home and requested her to prepare and fry a large bowl of fish. Inspite of it being uncharacteristic, the young woman obliged him by undertaking the onerous task of cleaning and frying the fish. He returned later that day to collect them, at which time he offered her no explanation; neither did she ask him for one. The next day, being Sunday, when he had failed to visit his children, his absence went unnoticed. With Denise being unwell again, the young woman was preoccupied in taking her to hospital for treatment.

Later that week, news of Mr Horton's marriage would permanently change Miss Mae's opinion of him, and by extension, Rose-Anne's as well. She too now shared Miss Mae's disapproval of Mr Horton. With no possibility of marriage for her daughter, she made it quite clear to him that he was no longer welcome at her home.

"In this life, sometimes it's better to cut and run than to stay and bu'n (burn)," Miss Mae had firmly told her daughter.

Despite this most dissatisfactory state of affairs, the young woman felt it incumbent on her to contact Mr Horton to inform him of her imminent departure. She again did this covertly behind her mother's back. It would be their final visit together; needless to say, he required little encouragement.

Back and forth her tortured thoughts swirled round and round in her head, like the rings on a child's spinning top. She continued sitting alone on deck in this deep reverie.

The twinkling harbour lights now attracted her attention. They seemed to mirror those of the stars in the sky above; the verdant hills and mountains were still faintly visible on the horizon. A slight chill in the air caused her to shiver before; at length, she reluctantly stirred. Walking at a leisurely pace past a few remaining passengers, who were chatting amiably together, she made her way carefully down a narrow staircase to her tiny cramped cabin, where she kicked off her shoes.

"Where yu a go, Mummy? Can we come with yu?"

She covered her ears with her hands in an attempt to blot out the haunting sound of her children's voices. The pain the young woman felt in that instance was overpowering. She broke down and cried until she felt numb.

CHAPTER 6

Secluded for long hours in her cabin, and with more than a sufficiency of time on her hands, the young woman grew tired and restless. The endless days at sea with no sign of land on the horizon merged seamlessly into one.

In this unvarying landscape, with her mind still in turmoil, she returned to thinking about Thadius. Her conscience was uneasy due to her treatment of him. Miss Mae's refusal to consent to their marriage led to him being ever more determined to change her mind. He left Jamaica to work on a farm programme in West Virginia. The work was demanding, and it involved him labouring outdoors in the fields for long hours. To demonstrate his commitment to the young woman and their daughter, Jumokah, Thadius sent Miss Mae his first wage packet. He asked her permission to build a separate room onto the main house for her daughter's comfort. Miss Mae approved his proposal, and in due course, the room was built. In the meantime, he kept the young woman updated on his circumstances.

"The wages are good," he told her. "I am working flat out to save sufficient money to pay down a deposit on a house for us. Please, give me another two years, and I will marry you and prove your mother wrong."

His plans and the assured knowledge that they would reunite in the near future did much to sustain Thadius. It gave him the inner strength to endure the hardship. He was so proud of the young woman and their daughter. His love for them was often reaffirmed in his letters.

It was, though, the unfortunate repercussion from a disquieting conversation between him and a work colleague, Jason Brownton from Trinidad, that would emphatically change the course of Thadius's life. Jason, who privately envied Thadius's good fortune, decided to play devil's advocate by asking him about his woman.

"You really believe se your woman faithful to you while you up here slaving away for she? I bet you any money she have another man!"

The question caught Thadius off-guard. He was shocked. It had never occurred to him to think such a thing of the young woman. Naturally, he spoke out staunchly in her defence. But as the seeds of doubt festered in his mind, it became an all-consuming thought which began eating him alive until he could think of nothing else. It was imperative that he learned the truth, so he set about writing to ask her if she was indeed seeing another man.

Thadius was extremely troubled by her response. His dream of marrying her disintegrated to dust. He could find no conciliatory words to describe his feelings for her in that moment of truth. He blamed himself for being delusional. Not only had she been seeing another man, but he learned from her they had two children. Her overt betrayal of him caused him to feel bitterly hurt and angry. What an absolute fool she had made of him. This he could not easily forgive. He saw little point in carrying on working for their future life in America, so he resigned from his job and returned to Jamaica with no clear plan in mind.

With few options open to him in Jamaica, Thadius eventually decided to join the armed forces in Britain. He was still in an emotionally charged state when he arrived at the young woman's home to bid farewell to his daughter Jumokah before leaving the island. Struggling to maintain his composure, it was a difficult meeting, which was made worse by Mr Horton's unexpected arrival. Thadius was so incensed at the sight of him, he gave vent to weeks of pent up frustration and anger. A dreadful fight ensued in the yard between the two men. He sprang at Mr Horton with the lightning speed of a black panther, easily collaring him in a headlock. Thadius, being the taller of the two, had a clear advantage over Mr Horton. He proceeded to punch him relentlessly in the head until blood streamed unchecked from his nose. He released him only when he was violently pulled back and restrained by the young woman's two brothers. Thadius turned on his heels and stormed angrily away from the house slamming the gate forcefully as he left, leaving everyone stunned. Some two decades would pass before their paths crossed again.

CHAPTER 7

As the ship *Asdania* forged its way across the Atlantic, the young woman emerged from her cabin early one morning to stand on deck. Shading her eyes with her hands, she scanned the horizon. Her heart skipped a beat on seeing the faint outline of land ahead. This was the first clear indication that her long journey was drawing to a close. Her eyes tracked the turbulent white trail of foaming waves the ship left in its wake as it sliced energetically through the choppy sea. It was somehow evocative of her own life.

After three wearisome weeks at sea she was hugely relieved to touch down on British soil. The motherland she had learned so much about at school. The young woman disembarked from the *Asdania* feeling liberated and ready to face her new life. A surge of optimism swept over her, lifting her mood. She was met at Southampton docks by Frances Green, a genteel, grey-haired woman from the hospital's medical team.

At their initial introduction, Frances briefed the young woman on the nursing training programme. She also recounted the history of the hospital where she would undertake her studies, explaining to her that the hospital had originally been established to deal with infectious diseases by the council in 1890. Under the health service, its expanded role now included the treatment of tuberculosis. A training school for nurses also came under the auspices of the hospital. For obvious reasons, Frances refrained from discussing with the young woman the disconcerting fact that many nurses had succumbed to the scourge of tuberculosis and died within the first year of their training[1].

They walked briskly together across the wharf in an effort to keep warm and find her luggage. Having cleared customs, they boarded a steam train bound for the north of Britain. She gazed at the unfamiliar scene through the train window in wonderment. The train chugged along, releasing a thick cloud of black smoke from its funnel which billowed high into the sky. The dense, grey low-lying clouds sealed out any glimmer of sunlight or warmth. The trees, stripped of their leaves, looked stark and naked against the gloomy skyline. It was a distinct contrast to the lush plants and colourful tropical animal life found in abundance in the hills and mountains of Jamaica.

The young woman shivered as a deep chill coursed its way through her body. Her coat, which she had imagined would be substantial enough to keep her warm, lacked the requisite quality to protect her against the cold. Outside, a bitter January wind created an icy draft which penetrated through gaps in the train windows keeping her hands and thinly stockinged feet cool and uncomfortable. Continuing to gaze through the window at the bleak scenery, the young woman found her raised spirits temporarily dampened.

At length, the train reached its destination. Frances escorted her to the nurses' accommodation where she met some of the other trainees. The young woman unpacked her belongings and looked apprehensively around the shabby, minimally furnished, unheated bedroom that was to be her home. Sitting gingerly on the edge of the bed, she found herself yearning for her mother and aunt Rose-Anne, who had taught her countless practical skills, her three brothers and younger sister—even Papa Gustavia. Despite not being her father, she reflected fondly on his many kindnesses. She missed her children dreadfully and she could only imagine their familiar noisy, lively play, and laughter which would ring out daily in the yard. She longed for the warmth of the sunshine, now more than ever before. She craved for her mother's unrivalled cooking, which served only to remind her that the food on board the ship had mostly been inedible. She imagined herself sniffing the delicate fragrant roses in the front garden. Even the stench from burning rubbish daily in the yard would have been welcomed. It was difficult for her to accept that she would not wake up to the sound of her cockerel crowing loudly at dawn or hear the dogs barking noisily together in the neighbourhood. What of the aroma of fully ripened mangoes, its sweet juice running down her chin? When would she be likely to eat a freshly picked mango in this cold country that had trees without any leaves? What would she not give to be back in Jamaica. But more than anything else in the world, she was fearful for her youngest daughter Denise. In that moment of deliberation, she realised that until now she had taken everything in her life for granted.

CHAPTER 8

In accordance with hospital protocol, the young woman attended an interview and induction session with matron which went well. At the meeting, she was given a weekly schedule to familiarise herself with the demanding hospital routine. In next to no time, she became attuned to her nursing studies, which had included eight weeks at training school, where she had taken copious notes on the theory of nursing—anatomy, hygiene, and nutrition amongst other medical topics. Thankfully for her, the daily hospital regime, which was strictly controlled by matron, turned out to be less daunting than she had initially anticipated. The young woman was overjoyed to make new friends with trainee nurses from the African colonies. In particular, the lifelong friendship she went on to form with Rosemary Grant, who too was Jamaican, would remain solid throughout their distinguished nursing careers.

Over the seasonal holiday period, the hospital allowed the trainees some latitude from the constraint of their nursing duties to socialise at dances held in a nearby community hall. Swept along by the music, and with no shortage of pretty party dresses, the young woman, who was an extremely able dancer, proved to be popular on the dance floor.

CHAPTER 9

Denise

At four years of age, Denise was a bright, articulate, and sometimes mischievous child who was naturally curious with an innate sense of fun. She particularly liked working out puzzles. Her mother was constantly searching for new ones to challenge her ability. It was unfortunate, though, that from birth, she often suffered from painful episodes emanating from her tiny swollen joints. Following a series of diagnostic tests carried out when she was two and a half years old, it was confirmed that Denise had sickle cell anaemia. Doctors knew very little about the disease or its effects at the time, and it was agreed that her condition should be treated conservatively.

Consistent with her secretive personality, the young woman chose not to discuss Denise's illness with her family. Instead, she placed her confidence in the doctors' ability to find a solution which she hoped would permanently resolve Denise's health problems. Unaware of this, Miss Mae was kept in ignorance of the severity of her granddaughter's condition.

The young woman impatiently looked forward to receiving updates on her children's progress and local news from Miss

Mae. In her most recent letter, sent in March 1955, she wrote that the children and the rest of the family were all in good spirits. Miss Groves, the children's teacher, had given an excellent report. Denise, in particular, was doing exceptionally well at school. She had been impressed with her reading, which had shown much improvement for her age. Jumokah was commended for her consistent work across all subjects, but Delton, she pointed out, continued to struggle with mathematics.

"Yes, my dear," Miss Mae continued in her letter. "Every change in Jamaica is big news, so you can imagine the excitement when it was reported in the Sunday newspaper that oil drilling was due to commence in Septuagint Bay. The possibility of generating our own home-grown income through oil production has added credence to the ever-increasing possibility of Jamaica becoming an independent country in the near future. Furthermore, the outcome of much discussion has led to the seal being set on Caribbean unity, with the establishment of a federation firmly agreed. Well, who would have believed such a thing would ever come about? The growers are in worries again, and they are seeking a new coconut deal."

The young woman hungrily devoured the content of the letter, reading and re-reading the pages. The news fortified and calmed her anxious spirit.

CHAPTER 10

Within barely four months of her arrival in Britain, a tragic sequence of events occurred in Jamaica. It began when Denise was happily playing tag with her two older siblings close to an outside kitchen in the yard. A heavy Dutch pot, which was balanced precariously on the edge of a makeshift zinc table, fell onto her foot causing a deep cut to her toe. Her painful scream sent Miss Mae and Rose-Anne running from the house and across the yard. Over the next few days, the wound was cleaned and bandaged and redressed a number of times. Yet, despite Miss Mae's very best efforts using herbal remedies, by the end of the week, it was clear from her rising temperature and continued discomfort that Denise's toe was not healing. Worse still, it was now severely infected.

Miss Mae duly tasked her youngest daughter Neena, to take Denise to the central hospital in Kingston for treatment. This was not an uncommon practice in a West Indian household with older children. They were occasionally expected to undertake responsibility for their younger siblings.

Unaware of Denise's previous medical history held on record at the children's hospital, the doctor's proceeded to treat the infection promptly. Penicillin was prescribed as the treatment of choice. A full dose was intravenously administered in a single shot, and Denise fell into a coma.

The rapid culmination of events that ensued threw the whole family into complete disarray. Miss Mae recoiled in sheer disbelief when she visited Denise in hospital. Her rapidly deteriorating condition left her blaming herself for not personally assuming charge of the initial hospital visit. She was pivotal to ensuring that her granddaughter was transferred to the children's hospital, where her entire medical history was made available to doctors treating her condition. The family were confused and surprised to learn that Denise had a history of sickle cell anaemia. It was also confirmed that she should never have been administered penicillin as part of her treatment plan. Never before had Miss Mae felt so irritated and frustrated by her daughter's habitual secretiveness.

CHAPTER 11

Over in Britain, a separate drama was unfolding. The young woman was very conscious that her latest pregnancy, resulting from her last intimate encounter with Mr Horton, was one secret it was impossible for her to keep hidden. There was no alternative for her but to request a meeting with matron to discuss her position. As she stood in the corridor outside matron's office, her heart pounded incessantly in her chest, the sound of which reverberated like a clashed cymbal throughout her body. She knocked timidly on the door.

"Come in," matron called out in her clear, distinct voice.

Sucking in a deep mouthful of air, she expelled it softly and slowly through her nostrils as she cautiously opened the door. Matron, who had her own suspicions that something was amiss, was thankful she had taken the initiative to come and see her.

Motioning with an outstretched arm, she invited the young woman to be seated. She perched uncertainly on the edge of a chair opposite matron's desk, wishing fervently that it would swallow her up. Her mouth felt dry as she attempted to explain her reason for being there. In due course, she found the words to explain that she was pregnant. Matron listened sympathetically. The young woman felt so deeply ashamed and anxious as she spoke. The room suddenly felt stiflingly warm, and tiny beads of perspiration formed across her forehead. She wiped the sweat away with a tiny handkerchief she was clutching in her hand. Matron leaned forward to kindly offer her a glass of water.

The young woman who was sitting uncomfortably in front of her now had caught her attention and impressed her right from her interview. Matron had instinctively sensed her keenness and enthusiasm to learn the job. Throughout her training she had demonstrated due diligence and commitment. Her attendance at lectures and her patient record-keeping throughout her work experience on the wards were meticulous and well above average. She had passed her basic training with ease. She was now a probationer nurse preparing for her exams at the end of her first year. Matron was under no illusion; she recognised how difficult it was for these student nurses from the Commonwealth countries to cope with being hundreds of miles away from their homes and families. It was regrettable that for a few of the girls it ended this way. A wave of annoyance swept over her. She had confidence in the young woman's ability to attain a State Registered Nurse (SRN) qualification. *Can these girls not see what a great chance they are throwing away* she thought angrily to herself. In her frustration, her first instinct was to get rid of the problem and arrange for her immediate extradition to Jamaica.

Before any action could be taken, for clarification, there were some uncomfortable truths that would have to be discussed. Matron went on to say to the young woman.

"We will have to consider the possibility of returning you to Jamaica. As you can see, we have no facilities here to accommodate a baby. Your circumstances will most certainly interfere with your training." She proceeded to ask her, "Is the father of your expected baby a local man?"

The young woman swallowed before mumbling that he lived in Jamaica and that she was already pregnant when she had arrived in Britain. She broke down sobbing, fitful, heartrending tears. She went on to explain to Matron that if her mother had known of the pregnancy she would never have allowed her to participate in the training programme. She knew how perilously close she was to losing her only chance to succeed in the one thing she had dreamt of since her childhood. How could she let it go now? In desperation, she pleaded with matron. As she spoke, her vulnerability became ever more transparent. Again matron had to muster all of her strength to control her exasperation. Speaking somewhat coldly, she added, "I will have to contact your family for a full discussion on your options."

The young woman shrank involuntarily even further back into the seat, in a vain attempt to protect herself from the impact of matron's words, which struck like a blow to her cheek. Her eyes widened fearfully. She did not want to return to Jamaica, not like this. What would Miss Mae and the rest of the family think of her? Acutely conscious that she had already let them down, it was with deep mortification that she could only imagine how they would receive the news of her latest pregnancy. The shame and humiliation of returning home a failure with yet another child was unbearable. Salty tears burned deep into the socket of her eyes, forcing her to lower her head as she sobbed silently, which caused her body to softly undulate. She made one further impassioned plea to matron not to send her back home.

Matron spoke softly but firmly as she reiterated her position, leaving the young woman under no misapprehension.

"The decision to send you home is highly probable, but I am unable to proceed without your parent's consent or approval."

Moving forward to more practical details, matron discussed with her the next steps to be taken.

"I will make an appointment with Dr Clark to carry out the required pregnancy tests. Then we can meet again to discuss where we go from here."

They spoke quietly together for a while. Consideration was given to the possible option of her going into a mother and baby home. Matron also promised to contact a children's home she thought might be able to accommodate the baby. At the conclusion of their meeting she was dismissed. The young woman slipped silently like a vapour of mist from the room.

Matron sat at her desk silently weighing up the pros and cons. She felt torn. Her primary role was to act in "loco parentis" to the girls in her care, which she did in earnest. Determined not to be judgemental of the young woman's unfortunate predicament, but rather to deal with the matter fairly and pragmatically, she drove away from her mind any negative thoughts. It was important, however, that she apprised the family of the young woman's changed circumstances; therefore, she sent them a telegram forthwith.

Two very serious question raised by the circumstances had left matron feeling uncomfortable, even as they persisted in her mind. Who would provide adequate foster care for a black baby? And how could she best protect the young woman from the stigma of the illegitimate birth of her baby? It was an established fact that births arising outside of wedlock were frowned upon by society; they were even considered by the Church to be sinful. Even if the father of the unborn child had been in a position to marry her, according to hospital rules in force at the time, she would have had to leave the nursing profession. Matron was determined, therefore, to follow through on her suggestion and organise affairs, keeping in mind the welfare of the unborn baby. If successful, it would at least afford the young woman the chance to finish her nursing training.

CHAPTER 12

In Jamaica, the family were close to breaking point. They felt powerless as they witnessed Denise's short life irretrievably draw to a close. On the last few occasions that she remained lucid, Denise quoted comforting scriptures from the Bible, a book she dearly loved and drew personal comfort from. Despite her tender age, her tranquil demeanour belied her uncanny perception of her impending death, which she accepted and was unafraid to meet.

"Lord, please commit me unto thine hands," she whispered as she inexorably slipped into deep unconsciousness.

At the tender age of four, on 2 May 1955, Denise Opal Horton died.

The nine-night ceremony which followed was attended by the entire Connor Town community. From 8 p.m., nine days after Denise's death, family, friends, and neighbours assembled at Miss Mae's home to support her through this altogether distressing event. By sharing Denise's brief childhood memories, they consoled the grieving family. It was undoubtedly a sad fact that the music they played and the food and drink they consumed offered little solace. The funeral took place a few days later.

"Ashes to ashes, dust to dust. The Lord giveth and the Lord taketh away."

In the oppressive heat of the midday sun, the priest's words rang out clearly in the cemetery above the sound of wailing mourners at the graveside. A tiny wooden coffin adorned with white lilies was gently lowered into a freshly dug grave. The women, who were soberly dressed in black, raised their voices high and mournfully sang "Rock of Ages."

Miss Mae led the procession of mourners as they filed past the tiny grave and threw down lumps of damp soil onto the coffin. The funeral macabrely took her right back to her own daughter Betty, who had died aged six years old from a serious accident which she sustained when climbing a tree. She too was buried at that cemetery. It vividly brought back the nightmare of losing yet another young child, leading Miss Mae to question God's true purpose for mankind. Why did innocent children have to suffer the pang of death in this way? Miss Mae determinedly wiped away her tears of grief as she supported herself on her husband's arm.

The funeral left Miss Mae feeling overwrought. She refused to respond to repeated knocks on her bedroom door, encouraging her to come out. Papa Gustavia feared for his wife's sanity. Drinking deeply from a large glass of white rum, he too recalled that on the occasion of Betty's death, Miss Mae was perceived by everyone to have lost her mind. Such was the depth of her anguish. Distraught, she was often brought home by relatives in a pitiable state from the cemetery where she had cried for hours at the grave of her dead child. The family anxiously prayed that this would not prompt a reoccurrence of that event.

Miss Mae remained sequestered in a darkened bedroom for several hours, refusing to face the family. She was unable to see how she would ever come to terms with the loss of her granddaughter.

She agonised over the undertaking of having to inform her daughter of Denise's death. In the end, she summoned all her strength to bravely emerge and send her daughter a telegram.

Alone in her room, on receipt of Miss Mae's telegram, the young woman collapsed as she read the devastating news of Denise's death. She was inconsolable. Engulfed by an overwhelming sense of grief and sorrow, she bitterly blamed herself for not being there. She questioned her mother's ability to perhaps have done more. With her hands clasped tightly around her extended stomach, she hugged herself, continuously rocking back and forth she found no comfort. She felt her unborn baby kicking her from within the hidden depths of her womb. It was a stark reminder that in the midst of death, new life existed. Agonising tears of woe streamed unchecked down her cheeks. In this, her darkest hour, she had never felt so wretched.

CHAPTER 13

With her enquiries finalised, in the remaining five weeks of her pregnancy, the young woman was invited by matron to accompany her on a visit to a children's home. They met with a senior member of staff who provided them with a potted history of the home. They learned that a nursery had been established there in 1944, and its overall accommodation comprised of forty cots in four wards. The home facilitated children ranging in age from babies to young teenagers. Matron felt reassured to see that a black baby girl was resident there. Another member of staff took them on a tour of the home and outside grounds. It was clean and sterile. The sparsely furnished wards contained beds and cots neatly spread with fresh white bed linen and covered with two thick grey woollen blankets. In the garden, children had access to a climbing frame, sandpit, and tricycles for outdoor play activities. Over the summer months they were taken on holiday to various seaside resorts along the coast. Babies swathed in warm shawls were placed outside in large prams to sleep for at least two hours daily regardless of weather conditions.

Matron took the young woman aside, where they discussed her first impression of the home. She felt reassured it would offer the right solution for her baby. The final details were left in matron's hands, subject to Miss Mae's approval. This was received in due course by matron, which meant the young woman would be able to continue her nursing training after the baby's birth. However, it was unfortunate that throughout the course of their discussions, all parties concerned failed to appraise the long-term ramifications of raising a child in an institutionalised environment.

CHAPTER 14

Demetria

On 31 July 1955, the young woman screamed in agony as she gave birth to her fourth child, whom she named Demetria. At barely six weeks old, she placed her baby in the home to resume her training. By virtue of the demands of her work schedule, from the outset, the young woman became distanced from her baby. With a round trip to the home taking approximately four hours, there was hardly sufficient time at those visits on her days off for a loving relationship or strong bond to develop between mother and daughter.

As she matured, Demetria's insecurities progressively worsened and began to impact negatively on her behaviour. Staff at the home reportedly found her belligerent, headstrong, and challenging to manage. Matters came to a head one lunchtime when she was five years old. She was injured by a member of staff, who in a misguided attempt to curtail her unruly behaviour, threw a spoon at her from across the table. It struck her forcefully in the face. Demetria was dazed and confused as blood trickled down her cheek, dripping slowly onto the table. She had sustained a deep painful cut above her right eye which was severe enough to warrant being stitched at hospital. The shaken staff member, fearing the reprisal from her action, had regrettably failed to make the connection that the underlying cause for Demetria's difficult behaviour was exacerbated by the separation anxiety she experienced on the occasions her mother visited the home. She was, in fact, growing into an angry and unhappy little girl. Incensed by the incident, uncharacteristically, the young woman wrote to Miss Mae to ask her advice. She responded by suggesting to her daughter that perhaps this might be an opportune time to think about reuniting her family. Particularly in view of the communication she had recently received from matron which advised her of her daughter's successful completion of her nursing training. She had attained a State Registered Nurse (SRN) qualification.

Immediate arrangements were put in hand for Miss Mae to travel to Britain in July 1961. She was accompanied on her journey by Delton and Jumokah. Much to her disgust, when she visited Demetria at the home, her Negroid hair had been shorn off leaving her looking like a boy. The staff there had no knowledge of how to handle her tight, curly hair. Neither could she help but notice the cut embedded over her right eye lid. Without further delay, Miss Mae removed Demetria from the home. At the earliest juncture, the young woman wound up her affairs at the hospital she had grown to love. She bid matron and her colleagues a fond adieu to join her children and Miss Mae in east London.

Some years later, Mr Horton commented on that phase of Demetria's life in a letter he wrote to her in 1980.

"Again, my heart bleeds for your deprived and lost childhood, and I feel ill at the notion that you have inherited such an empty period of history."

CHAPTER 15

In London, the family lived in rented accommodation within walking distance of a vibrant local street market. With three children and two adults crowded into a small two-bedroomed flat, tensions often flared up between the children. Delton and Jumokah, who were unused to being confined for long hours indoors, hankered after their aunt Rose-Anne and spacious outdoor yard, where they were used to playing daily. The children were overwhelmed by an unfamiliar school system, change in climate and living with their mother after a separation which had lasted several years. Demetria fared the best out of the three children. She heartily embraced her family, which had given her security and a sense of attachment. This feeling was reinforced through the firm and loving relationship, which continued to grow between her and Miss Mae. She also had a good rapport with her brother, Delton. Sadly, however, such was not the case with Jumokah her eldest sister. Their eight-year age gap and years of living apart had regrettably left its mark on their relationship.

Miss Mae continued to practically support her daughter by caring for her children. This allowed her to continue in her nursing career, where she had chosen to specialise in paediatric nursing. She became extremely proficient in the care of sick young children and babies.

A solution to alleviate the overcrowding at the family's accommodation was worked out by Miss Mae when she approached her brother, Stanley, who lived alone in west London in a large three-bedroom flat above a carpet shop. He agreed to her moving into his flat with Delton and Demetria. Although this resolved the problem, the family were again separated.

CHAPTER 16

The early 1960s saw the young woman briefly married to a mature Nigerian law student. For a number of reasons, her marriage came to be one of the unhappiest points of her life, leaving her nursing career at a total standstill. She gave birth to three children for her husband in quick succession, one of which was a stillborn baby girl. The emotional strain took its toll on her health leaving her depressed. In addition, divergences arising from her husband's cultural background proved insurmountable. These were the primary cause of discord between them. Her marriage subsequently ended in divorce leaving her feeling utterly dejected and struggling to cope with her family responsibilities.

She was invited to jointly run a private residential children's home. The proposal was appealing, as it would give her much needed capacity to manage her family commitments whilst running the home. She invested hours of her time and money setting up the project, only to discover that the co-director of the home had defrauded the business by embezzling advance childcare fees paid by parents even before the first intake of children. The legal issues arising from winding up the company took several months to resolve.

After a short spell of recuperation, she returned to nursing, where she took on a challenging role at a hospice which offered specialised, compassionate, palliative care for terminal patients. Immersing herself once again in nursing was sufficient to re-ignite her passion; she was back to doing what she loved best. Whilst working at the hospice, the young woman availed herself of training opportunities to increase her knowledge and develop valuable skills in other fields of nursing.

During the 1970s, the health service was subject to changes within its structure that would test her commitment to the nursing profession. She became increasingly disillusioned and discouraged by inconsistencies within the organisation. Imposed cuts to a range of services negatively affected the quality of patient care nurses were expected to deliver. She was forced to concede that her nursing career had reached a stalemate. How she longed for a change of direction. Even as she was pondering her choices she received an intriguing call.

CHAPTER 17

Thadius, whom she had not seen since he left Jamaica in the 1950s, contacted her. He was visiting Britain from the United States, where he now lived. Feeling adventurous, the young woman agreed to meet up with him. She had nothing to lose; furthermore, they were both divorcees. For a short while, it seemed their renewed whirlwind romance would blossom and have a magical happy ending. Thadius's presence generated great expectations from amongst family members, especially, when in a grandiose gesture, he presented the young woman with a stunning diamond ring. He declared that his love for her had never died. The attention he lavished gave her confidence a much-needed boost, but it was insufficient to change the outcome. The direction their lives had taken had permanently changed who they were, and sadly they were no longer on the same page. Time for them had not stood still. Their daughter, Jumokah, also demanded her share of his attention too, which gave rise to tension between the young woman and her daughter. Issues that enamated from this triangulated affair in the end served only to restrict its growth. Commitment to a long-term relationship was ultimately ruled out by both parties. Consequently, as it had begun, the affair ended without recourse. In spite of this, they did remain loyal lifelong friends.

Then out of the blue on a bitterly cold day in December 1974, her very good friend and nursing colleague, Rosemary Grant, called in to see her on one of her days off.

"Guess what," Rosemary told her. "I have information, on good authority, that a recruitment company from Texas is seeking to employ SRN-qualified British nurses. I thought it might be ideal for us to give it a try. What do you think, are you up for it?"

They talked together long into the evening. The chance was music to her ears; and could be the change she was seeking. They both applied and were accepted onto the scheme without hesitation. Prior to moving to the States permanently, the young woman spent one year there familiarising herself with the country before she immigrated in 1977, accompanied by her three youngest sons. A condition of her divorce resulted in her two youngest children from her marriage being made Wards of Court. She refused to let this stand in her way. Instead, she removed them illegally from the country to start a new life for her family. Her three adult children remained in Britain, free to make their own way in life.

At 50 years of age, it was a courageous move. The States opened up a whole new world of opportunities for her. She bought her own home in a pleasant neighbourhood. She learned to drive, accomplishing it all unsupported as a single parent responsible for three teenage boys. She made friends with an affable couple, who lived across the street, Jasmine and Regan Mills. Their boys were of a similar age and the two families got on well together.

A pivotal event occurred towards the end of a particularly stressful week at work. Twin babies she had been nursing were critically ill and their prognosis was uncertain. While still feeling tense and worried in connection with the twins, Jasmine had called to invite her over to a party that coming Saturday. She reluctantly accepted, as it was the last thing she felt like doing. When she arrived at the party, the room was buzzing with lively activity from around twenty couples packed into the living room. Jasmine and Regan were in high spirits, as the music blared loudly from the speakers. Regan handed her a glass of iced tea and introduced her to Gregory Melford, a close family friend. *Rock the boat* was the next tune to hit the turntable and Gregory asked her to dance. Not only was he a fantastic dancer, there was an instant attraction between them. They agreed at the end of the evening to keep in touch with eath other, which they did. From the outset, it was apparent to her that she had finally met her soulmate. It simply felt right when Gregory asked her to marry him. She accepted without hesitation, thus putting the seal on a happiness she never ever dreamed she would experience. When Rosemary Grant attended their wedding, she could not stop beaming from ear to ear.

"At last my dear friend", she whispered in her ear. "At last. You know that having a fulfilling working life is one thing, but to be happy in your personal life is quite another. I just know that Gregory Melford is right for you." She walked over to him with tears of joy sparkling in her eyes.

"Take good care of her" she gently cautioned him whilst genially shaking his hand.

"Come on over here Mrs Grace Melford" said Gregory, his face aglow as he drew her protectively into his arms.

CHAPTER 18

A key highlight from her early nursing career, in the period when tuberculosis was still prevalent worldwide, she was rewarded to witness one of the first children she had ever nursed, survive treatment for pulmonary tuberculosis. The disease was still prevalent worldwide in the 1950s. Much of the child's treatment involved her recovering from the debilitating affects of the disease in an iron lung, which enabled her to breathe when she lost her normal muscle function. By November 1956, the child was well enough to celebrate her fifth birthday out of the iron lung, much to the joy of her family and hospital staff. The child's recovery had a profound affect on the young trainee nurse. It gave her definitive proof and affirmed that her nursing skills really could make a difference to someone's life.

According to Mr Horton, who sardonically wrote in a letter to Demetria, that it took her mother up to "the evening of a whole lifetime to fix herself up". She certainly did "fix herself up" to overcome countless adversities. She officially retired from what had been a most gratifying professional nursing career in 1994, where, beyond a shadow of a doubt, she had been highly respected, by consultants and colleagues alike, many of whom she had worked with closely for several years. She never forgot that her mother's insightful encouragment to follow her interest enabled her to fulfil her childhood dream of becoming a nurse. Sadly, she died from cancer in February 1988.

The loss through death of two of her daughters, are aptly encapsulated in an extract from "I Shed One Tear", a moving poem by Jamaican poet Calvin Ckerr.

"Seeing the Mother, choked by sadness,
She's burying her daughter feeling like
She's the only one in the world. So I shed one tear.
This life ain't about all happiness
It's about sadness too
So I shed one tear, only for the children."

MR HORTON

One secret of success in life is for a man
to be ready for when his opportunity comes.
—Benjamin Disraeli

CHAPTER 1

When Mr Horton had stood on the pier at Kingston Harbour, wistfully watching the mother of two of his children board the *Asdania*, he knew then with no uncertainty that he had missed an opportunity. Yet he felt jealous of her freedom to leave the island, despite having taken the decision not to marry her. He had chosen instead to deal illicitly with her, knowing fully well that he offered her no long-term future. His actions had exposed his self-interested involvement with her, for which he was now paying a high price. He had been ostracised from her family, who wanted nothing more to do with him. His presence at Miss Mae's home was merely tolerated for the sake of his children Delton and Denise.

His troubles would not end there. Shortly after her arrival in Britain, Mr Horton learned from the young woman that she was expecting their third child. This was unwelcome news. His existing finite resources were already stretched to the limit, balancing the needs of his wife, who was also pregnant with their fourth child.

Then the unthinkable occurred. The tragic loss of their daughter Denise shook his world apart like an earthquake. Never in his lifetime had he envisioned burying his own child before him. On the day of her funeral, looking drawn and ashen, he stood aloof as the funeral party assembled to watch Denise's tiny coffin being carefully lowered into the grave. Mr Horton joined them as they filed slowly past, the freshly dug grave. Some threw handfuls of damp earth which landed with a dull thud on top of the coffin and scattered loosely amongst the white lilies. He had no voice to sing with the rest of the mourners. Neither did he wish to socialise with them following the funeral. Denise's death had added an incredible weight to his already desolate outlook. His feelings were compounded by his inability to share his grief directly with the mother of his children or to give her much needed loving support.

In a touching gesture, he did reach out to her by means of sending her a gift. His daughter Demetria came across it years later, hidden away at the bottom of her mother's old trunk. In all probability, the parcel would have been handed to her mother by matron. A closer examination of the handwriting on the parcel would have caused her heart to quicken its pace. She would have opened it carefully, as did Demetria, to reveal, lovingly wrapped in soft white tissue paper, an ivory-coloured lace christening shawl that had been made for her new baby by Mr Horton's wife. This unexpected gesture strangely lifted her spirits. Yet, despite not being personally acquainted with Mrs Horton, it nevertheless helped to lessen her feelings of isolation and loneliness. A few weeks later, their baby daughter Demetria was born. On the occasion of her christening, the young woman again drew surprising comfort from Mrs Horton's gift when she swaddled her tiny baby in the shawl. Despondent from her grief and sorrow, she heard little of the Christening service; the priest's words were lost to her, transported out of earshot to the rafters of the church. The tiny infant stirred in her arms, reacting to the sensation of the holy water the priest had liberally sprinkled on her face. The young woman drew the shawl closer around the baby rocking her gently. Alone with no family members close by, she carried the burden of this new life with a heavy heart. She sought desperately to find comfort in the fact that the life of this baby would, she prayed, in some way counterbalance the loss of her daughter Denise. Would she be able to reconcile her feelings? She doubted that this would ever be the case.

CHAPTER 2

George Horton was born on 27 March 1927, in Jamaica. He was popularly known as Mr Horton. Demetria knew little of her father's early life, as there was a reticence on the part of her mother or grandmother, Miss Mae, to discuss him. His earlier dealings with the family had caused dissent amongst them.

Mr Horton's parents had died when he was in his early teens, leaving him with few options, other than to make his own way in life. Being an articulate and resourceful young man, he quickly learned to live by his wits and to avail himself of any opportunities or resources that came his way in order to survive. He supplemented his income by teaching evening classes at a local college. He spent his days working hard to build a career for himself in welding. His reputation was definitively trademarked through his innovative style and ability to fashion a piece of iron into something equally of beauty and practical value. His finished pieces expressed the heart and soul of his craft. Some of his handiwork still remains in use to this day, with one of his loveliest bespoke pieces being a contemporary wrought-iron ten-seater dining table with matching chairs.

Countless words could be used to describe Mr Horton, even though they might not all prove complimentary. No one was more conscious of this than he. Demetria was commended by him once for the restraint she had shown in not calling him by the many names that he so justly deserved. Despite his shortcomings, he encouraged her in his belief that respectful behaviour towards her mother and father was central to her achieving positive outcomes throughout her life.

Mr Horton's story could easily have been written from at least eighteen different perspectives, as that was the number of children he fathered between his wife, Demetria's mother, and at least two other women. It was his love of women that would challenge his veracity.

Demetria was nine years old when she first met Mr Horton and his family. Their relationship would strengthen in her teenage years when they began communicating in earnest through their mutual letter-writing.

CHAPTER 3

The complexity of Demetria's family history started to unravel, with 1961 being a key transitional phase of her life. It was notably marked by Miss Mae's removal of her from the only home she had known virtually since her birth to live with her mother, and older siblings, Delton and Jumokah. The family moved from the north of England to a modest two-bedroom flat in the east end of London. A popular, large, historical street market, dating back to Roman times, dominated the town centre.

Miss Mae was often heard to say that while Britain lacked Jamaica's sunshine, shopping in the market reminded her of the hustle and bustle of the outdoor markets found back home. Each week, when they shopped together, Miss Mae and Demetria would walk past a jellied eel shop, where slimy, wriggling live eels contained in long trays were freshly cooked and sold, alongside hot pie and mash. These enormously popular dishes were the east end of London's street food of its day. Demetria, for her part, was never tempted to eat any of them.

It was customary for Miss Mae to cook a generous pot of soup every Saturday. Her four other children, who also lived in London at the time, would visit her on the weekend. Demetria's favourite amongst them was her Aunt Neena and her cousin

Carla. In the evening, the family would gather round the dining table in convivial companionship to eat a huge, steaming bowl of her filling soup, regardless of the time of year. They would reminisce fondly together about their former life in Jamaica, sharing unforgettable memories of the times too numerous to mention, when Miss Mae would sew through the night to produce elegant dresses for her girls, on the occasions they were invited to attend private parties or dances with live bands held at the yatching club in Kingston. Escorted by their brothers, she ensured that her girls were stunning 'belles of the ball'. Cricket was a firm favourite with her boys. On test cricket match days, armed with amply-filled picnic baskets, along with a girl or two, they were proud to remember the cricket club's greatest moment, 365 not out, made by Gary Sobers. The realisation that these times would never return, emphasised the importance of these gatherings. It was her way of staying connected to her roots and maintaining precious contact with her family.

CHAPTER 4

Reminiscing on the past, as she occasionally did, began to affect Miss Mae. In the end, she admitted to her daughter that she was missing her husband, sister and her dressmaking business. In short, she was homesick. The long, cold British winters had tested her resilience, so she decided to return to Jamaica. Her daughter asked her to take along Delton and Demetria to live with their father. Delton could scarcely contain his glee when he was told of the forthcoming trip; he longed to see aunt Rose-Anne again. Demetria would finally meet her father in the flesh for the first time.

Miss Mae set about patiently completing her preparations for the lengthy trip by sea. She adamantly refused to fly on the iron bird, a term she used to describe an aeroplane. It was a mode of transport she greatly feared. On a dreary damp day in July 1964, they set sail from the port of Southampton. The ship made an initial stop in Madeira, where she and the children spent five pleasant hours on shore before reboarding the ship. From that point, it took a further eighteen harrowing days in open sea before they reached their final destination. Demetria suffered from severe seasickness the entire journey. She managed to survive on a meagre diet of jelly and ice cream. It was a most welcome relief to disembark at Kingston Harbour, where the ill effects of the arduous journey were almost immediately dispelled at the sight of a gloriously bright, sunny day.

Demetria's initial impression of Jamaica as she had walked unsteadily down the gang plank of the ship, clutching a bag that contained her favourite blue-eyed blonde doll, was how warm the sun felt on her skin. The clear, sky and surrounding sea were deep shades of blue and bore no resemblance to that of foggy, damp London. She had to squint to protect her eyes from the unaccustomed brightness of the sunlight. She was in awe, never before had she been surrounded by such a large number of black people of every conceivable shade. She learned later, that when placed in their proper historical context, due to ties with Africa, Britain, Germany, Ireland, East and South Asia, and Spain, there were an array of terms which could be used to describe the hair type and skin colour of Jamaican people. They were a mixture of several cultures. Collectively, though, they were defined, according to the precept of the country's national motto, as one people.

Papa Gustavia and Rose-Anne were at the wharf to meet them. It was a most joyous reunion with tears of gladness shed by them all. Papa Gustavia eagerly helped to load all the luggage into a waiting taxi. He had sorely missed his wife. Demetria felt a light breeze blow directly off the sea, it gently rustled the leaves of the palm trees that lined the beach close to the harbour. Its cooling effect was most welcome. The sand on the beach was dark grey in colour and quite unlike the white sandy beaches she would later see on the north coast of the island.

The family proceeded to drive from the harbour towards Connor Town. On route, Demetria was again fascinated by the brightly dressed black people and children she saw out on the dry, dusty streets, either playing football and cricket, swimming, or fishing in the sea. She had been similarly intrigued by the street vendors. Their wooden carts were loaded with fresh seasonal fruits, the likes of which she had never seen before, such as deep red Otaheiti apples, dew plums, fragrant Jack fruit, and coconuts, still tightly encased in their thick green husks. Miss Mae stopped the taxi to buy coconuts for everyone from one of the vendors. The vendor deftly chopped through the husks using a long, sharp, cutlass to create an opening on the top of the coconut. Greedily sipping the pale, creamy, almost translucent liquid through a straw, Demetria took an instant dislike to her first taste of coconut water; she just wanted to spit it out.

CHAPTER 5

Two days after her arrival in Jamaica, Demetria suffered a major asthma attack. She was unfortunate enough to celebrate her ninth birthday in hospital. It was while she was there that she first met her father. Being far too unwell to appreciate his visit, she was aware from his worried expression that he was concerned about her health. He visited her again shortly after she returned home. He was anxious for news on her progress. He also wanted to share some practical advice with Miss Mae regarding asthma. On this subject, he had her full attention.

"Please, Miss Mae, do anything in your power that will improve Demetria's general health. I am begging you to see to it that she does deep breathing exercises regularly with emphasis on blowing out when she is well. We already know that because of her asthmatic condition breathing is her problem. In my experience, I can tell you that only deep breathe-out exercises will help to mitigate any future episodes." She concurred, giving him a rare nod of approval.

It is interesting to note that Mr Horton's practical advice to Demetria would have almost certainly been discouraged by some doctors, on the grounds that there was insufficient evidence to prove that they really worked. Conversely, recent studies support the concept of a regime of breathing exercises, deeming that they might well improve a person's breathing and quality of life.[2]

Demetria carefully studied Mr Horton from her reclining chair on the veranda. He was much shorter than she had pictured in her mind. She found him to be friendly enough, although his low-cut hairline had receded further from his forehead than she remembered from photographs she had seen of him in Britain. He wore khaki-coloured pants and a matching short-sleeved shirt. Miss Mae fussed around her as she drew up a seat for him next to hers. Rose-Anne brought out a tray loaded with glasses of fresh lemonade and a large plate of banana fritters that she had fried earlier that morning. He helped himself to the refreshments. Demetria was inclined to be wary of him, not knowing quite how to react towards him, but in no time at all, he had set her at ease, effortlessly succeeding to draw her out in conversation. He soon realised that she was naturally talkative. From her observation she noted that his softly spoken speech was refined and eloquent.

He explained to her and Delton that he now had six children who were all looking forward to them joining his family. He discussed with Miss Mae the possibility of them moving to his home at the end of August before school restarted in September.

After he left, Demetria romantically pictured in her mind that his home would be a stately, beautiful white stucco two-story building, situated high up on a hill. She correctly guessed the location, for indeed her father's home was built on a hill. By the end of the summer holiday, she would discover what in actuality lay ahead.

CHAPTER 6

Demetria gradually learned more about her extended family. Miss Mae herself had been one of thirteen children, although several of her siblings were no longer alive. Her parents had died young, leaving her eldest sister, Rose-Anne, to raise the family. It meant she had missed out on the chance to marry. Miss Mae and Rose-Anne had always lived together, and because of this they were particularly close. Her remaining sister, Sissy, lived in a rented room in the vicinity of Connor Town. She was also the twin sister of her brother Stanley, who resided in London. Sissy was a thin, gregarious, and very kind woman. Neither twin were married nor had any children of their own. Consequently, she found nothing more pleasurable than spending time with Miss Mae's grandchildren. Sissy was notoriously fond of taking a nip of white rum, and she was often to be seen in good-humoured spririts at a local rum bar. Demetria came to associate her and Papa Gustavia with a noticeable smell of rum on their breath. Last but not least her brother, Moulton. Miss Mae was close to Moulton and his partner, Miss Laura. They lived within walking distance of Bloomberg Street. Whilst her nephew, Papa, lived just a few doors away from Miss Mae on the same street. Papa was a short, dapper man with wavy jet black hair that was always neatly trimmed. His wide smile revealed a gold cap on one of his upper front teeth. He was the local barber. His barbering skills also extended to the maintenance of the hedge bordering his front garden, which was notably immaculately shaped and trimmed.

At all hours daily, a constant stream of friends, family members, and neighbours would call in at Miss Mae's home; it was a busy, sociable hub. Dressmaking had always been her predilection. She loved designing and creating new outfits, and there was no bound to her inventiveness. The success of her business was endorsed by satisfied clients who repeatedly returned for fittings, to place fresh orders or collect their finished garments. Her sewing room was filled with pretty fabrics, laces, and a vast array of coloured cotton threads. Garments that were finished had to be pressed using a large heavy coal iron. To heat it up, she would open a lid on top of the iron where it was filled with small pieces of burning coal. Projects at various points of completion were draped neatly across her sewing machine or fitted over her vintage mannequin. Demetria was enthralled by the things she saw in that room.

The month of July marked the start of the school summer holiday. Demetria enjoyed the unaccustomed freedom of playing outside in the large open yard for long hours daily. Revelling in the company of her siblings and cousins, the children became close. Her general health improved from constant exposure to the sunshine and eating freshly prepared meals made from seasonal vegetables and herbs that were grown in Miss Mae's back garden.

CHAPTER 7

Demetria being an inquisitive girl with an enquiring mind was often to be seen positioned at the gate chatting casually with the postman, fish man, broom man, and a host of other neighbours that made up the Connor Town community. From her vantage point, she keenly observed their activities and learned much about their lives. She found herself drawn into family dramas which were openly played out in nearby yards. It was a way of life that she would formerly have been excluded from, living behind the privacy of closed doors in Britain. She was fascinated by the goings-on of Mr and Mrs Johnson, a middle-aged couple, who ran a local grocery store opposite Miss Mae's home. Mr Johnson left the shop most afternoons only to arrive home later drunk and in an argumentative state. Her feelings went out to Mrs Johnson as she listened to her husband goading her into retaliation. Then they would argue heatedly, swearing and shouting abusively at each other. As the disagreement reached its pinnacle, it was a much-humiliated Mrs Johnson who was left with no choice other than to close the shop. Demetria would hear Miss Mae sternly ordering her from the gate. Reluctantly she would tear herself away. The shutters were too thin to prevent the sound of the abusive and hurtful words that continued to be hurled back and forth between the couple long into the evening. In the morning, the shop would reopen when, for a short while at least, their world would resume a sense of normality.

She made friends with Gail from next door, where she spent untold amusing hours. Gail was the older of the two, and both girls clicked right from the start. Demetria was fascinated by Gail's Jamaican accent, and it was not long before she had firm command of the locally spoken patois. They would often laugh together at her attempts to mimic their neighbours in an exaggerated accent. The girls, who had little to give each other materially, generously shared their seasonal crops. On the occasion of Gail's birthday, Miss Mae surprised them with two lovely matching dresses. Gail could not have been happier.

Two houses up from the Johnson's shop, Demetria regularly observed a young lad, not much older than Delton, being frequently beaten in his yard for minor misdemeanours. His punishment would be harshly administered. She discerned from whispered conversations between Miss Mae and Rose-Anne, that his mother was working abroad. The relatives, who were supposedly caring for him in her absence, treated him unkindly. This, unhappily, was the fate of some children who were left in the care of unscrupulous relatives when their parents accepted work opportunities abroad. Demetria came to understand from those daily dramas that, sadly, physical and verbal abuse was commonly practised and tolerated in some households.

Ackee season created another welcome distraction for Demetria. There were four large ackee trees standing tall and proud in the back yard. At the season's height, Miss Mae, would call a small boy who lived two houses away to pick the fruit.

Demetria would watch, fascinated, as he shimmied nimbly up the tree trunk with the greatest of ease; it took him no time at all to pick the fruit. Rose-Anne was in charge of the laborious task of preparing them for cooking. She removed the yellow oval-shaped fruit from its red outer pod along with the seeds and inner red membrane. Demetria would willingly carry some to her uncle Moulton's house on the way to school. By lunchtime, he would have prepared her favourite meal, delicious ackee and saltfish. This was served, saturated in coconut oil, on top of a large dumpling he named a cartwheel. After lunch, she had her own chipped enamel mug, which she took to a nearby grocery store, where for a penny, she had it filled with sheared ice that was drenched in bright, sweet, red syrup. These delightful lunchtimes were to become indelibly printed in her mind. His partner, Miss Laura, would take care of her school uniform, seeing to it that her white blouses were washed and starched. She would iron the pleats in Demetria's skirt, making sure they were as stiff and straight as a set of cookery knives. Any issues at school were taken care of by either Miss Mae or her aunt Sissy. Occasionally, as a special treat, when Miss Mae had to shop for fabrics downtown, she would take Demetria along with her. Once their shopping was completed, Miss Mae would buy them a pattie. After they had eaten it, and washed it down with a fizzy drink, they would go to a wonderful ice cream parlour, where she would be allowed to indulge in a large helping of rum and raisin ice cream. Extended family life had its obvious benefits and Demetria flourished in this warm-hearted, caring environment. All the same, the wind of change had already begun to blow.

CHAPTER 8

The summer holiday flew by, and at the end of August, Demetria and Delton moved to Mr Horton's home. The journey there had to be the scariest trip she had ever experienced in her whole life. He came to collect them in a beat-up old open-backed truck, into which their belongings were loaded. Miss Mae and Sissy were seated in the front of the truck, next to the driver. Demetria was carefully wedged between Mr Horton and Delton on a makeshift seat at the rear of the truck. There was an odd assortment of old tools and crocus bags that slid back and forth on the floor as the truck moved at breakneck speed along the road towards the hills. At Mr Horton's shouted request to the driver, he made a quick stop at his welding shop. He returned to the truck carrying a large sack of chicken feed. The driver continued on their journey, riskily cutting in and out of his lane onto the direct path of oncoming traffic. Demetria could hear Miss Mae and her aunt Sissy taking it in turns to curse the driver for his reckless handling of the vehicle. Her hands felt clammy as the fright and nerves started building inside her. She had visions of the truck overturning or crashing headlong into an oncoming car.

"Ease up na, man. Yu a go kill we in here today," shouted Miss Mae.

"Yu na see we have two pickney in de back of de truck. Me say *mind de pickney dem*," hollered Sissy.

The driver swerved violently; he had narrowly missed an oncoming car by the breadth of a hair.

"*Lord God*," gasped Miss Mae. "A dat me a say, you out to kill we in ya today," she bawled at the driver.

Demetria screamed hysterically, overtaken by sheer panic when the truck jerked them unceremoniously from their makeshift seat. Mr Horton looked mortified as he tried to calm her down. He wrestled to take hold of the side of the truck while attempting to reposition them on the seat. He too strongly appealed to the driver, who was insensible to all their entreaties with regard to the safety of his passengers. When he braked sharply at the foot of a winding and narrow road which led to the sparsely populated area of Green Havenville, he had no choice other than to slow right down and apply extreme caution. The hills were fittingly named due to their generous covering of lush, thick green vegetation. They were host to a spectacular variety of wild birdlife, butterflies and rare orchids. A section of the road levelled out and spanned a short section of a river which could be crossed by means of an old wooden swing bridge. The rickety bridge swung in every direction as all types of vehicles rumbled over it increasingly weakening its ropes on every turn of the wheel. It did, however, offer a shorter route to Mr Horton's property, so the risk was considered worth taking. The truck laboured dangerously up the hillside, which had breathtaking sheer drops visible from either of its sides as it bobbed and weaved edgily around each hairpin bend. We stopped unceremoniously at the foot of a large wrought iron gate where Mr

Horton jumped nimbly out of the truck taking with him his sack of corn. He pulled opened the gate to reveal his house.

When she climbed out of the truck, Demetria was still trying to decide which had been worse, driving along the narrow road or crossing the swing bridge. But she was lost for words, so much so she was unable to express her utter disappointment as she viewed the unfinished structure that stood before them. This was to be her home. Her image of a white stucco two-story building that she had conjured up in her mind was instantly dispelled. The house that stood before her could only be described as a building project still very much in progress. Miss Mae and Sissy were also dumfounded. They each hastily exchanged puzzled glances which indicated they were singularly unimpressed. With dusk fast approaching, they remained long enough to meet the entire family, before tearfully taking their leave of the children. Demetria was pleasantly surprised to observe that the main living space contained colourful handmade cushions that brought unexpected warmth into the room—as did the children's artistic creations which adorned the walls, helping to soften the unfinished plasterwork.

The way of life in Green Havenville was remarkably sedate when compared with the cordial hustle and bustle of Miss Mae's home. Mrs Horton worked at a local bakery store on weekdays, while Mr Horton left early for work each day, returning home late from his endeavours in the evening. The property had no running water or electricity. Whilst a daily source of anxiety for Demetria was an outside pit toilet. Due to its design (basically the toilet being a deep hole in the ground connected to a toilet seat) it was prone to attract significant quantities of cockroaches and other insects. Using it could only be described as an unpleasant experience.

A pretty garden on the grounds filled with established fruit trees and bushes were lovingly tended to by Mrs Horton. They yielded abundantly; thus, she was amply rewarded for her efforts with an array of seasonal fruits and vegetables. Mr Horton raised chickens, rabbits, guinea pigs, and pigeons. The rabbits and chickens provided food for the table. Blossom from the Acacia trees was favoured by the bees and was one of Demetria's most enduring memories of her time spent at Mr Horton's house. At certain times of the year, determined by the bees, donned in a protective beekeeper's outfit and armed with a smoke gun to make the bees drowsy, he would harvest the honey from the bee hives. This light, clear Acacia honey was the most delightful Demetria had ever tasted in her life.

The garden became her sanctuary; it turned out to be the only place where she could submerge herself in the surrounding natural environment without interruption from anyone. It gave her a measure of solitude and tranquillity. Otherwise, privacy was a scarce commodity when ten people cohabitated together. They all ate and slept in the main living room, the most completed space in the house. At night, the room converted into one large bedroom. Various fold-out beds were spread around sections of the room. Pressured oil lamps were used to illuminate the space in the evening. These attracted moths, which fluttered their fragile wings against its external glass casing. Additional fluorescent lighting from glow-worms shone eerily from the walls after the lamps were turned off. The beds were neatly stacked and stored daily. The family showered and washed their clothes from water stored in a large outdoor tank. Water, being a precious commodity, was expected to be used conservatively.

With each passing day, Demetria missed living with Miss Mae. She spent her waking hours daydreaming and longing to return to her home. She became fretful and unhappy there, not because she was being ill-treated but she found it difficult to cope with the rigours of such an unconventional lifestyle.

CHAPTER 9

Miss Mae and Mr Horton had a disagreement during the run up to Christmas over a trip she had planned to take Delton and Demetria to see the annual Christmas pantomime. People from all over the island flocked to Kingston for this premier event. His refusal led to Sissy and Miss Mae removing her grandchildren from his house early in the New Year. Much to Demetria's surprise and great relief, she arrived there without prior warning when he was still at work. They demanded that the children's belongings be packed without delay, as she informed the family the children would be leaving. Needless to say, Miss Mae's course of action justifiably caused an even deeper rift in her already fractious relationship with Mr Horton. Demetria and Delton, on the other hand, were overjoyed to return to living at Miss Mae's home. Their rejoicing, though, proved to be short-lived.

CHAPTER 10

After spending just one eventful year in Jamaica, Demetria and Delton were bitterly disappointed to learn from Miss Mae that she was determined to return to Britain. She was at odds with Papa Gustavia, caused by his wanton drinking. Needless to say, Mr Horton was unable to influence her otherwise; hers was the final word on the matter. The breach between them was far from healed, but he was resolute in his determination to set aside his differences and see his children off at the airport. It was a bittersweet departure. On the one hand, Demetria would never forget her time in Jamaica; she had amassed an abundance of treasured memories. In particular, she had enjoyed being friends with Gail. They had faithfully vowed to write to each other when she returned to Britain, but somehow, they never again made contact. The time she had spent getting to know her father and extended family, albeit short, had been a priceless education and would shape various aspects of her future life. A part of her had missed the country of her birth — well, at least the easy things, like travelling on public transport and going to school. Delton and Demetria dutifully promised their father to continue in communication with him by letter.

They were met at the airport in London by their mother, who

was heavily pregnant. She looked stressed and tired. Demetria stayed with her and the rest of the family until Miss Mae arrived a few weeks later. It was agreed that Delton would remain with his mother. Demetria visited the family most weekends, but she took this latest upheaval and separation to heart. Yet, before long, she would learn that another major change was looming on the horizon.

Miss Mae's two youngest sons were in the process of moving to America to seek new challenges there. Her two daughters and eldest son and their children were by now reasonably settled in Britain. Her sister Rose-Anne, who had managed their home in Jamaica singlehandedly in her absence, had recently turned 75 years old. With that in mind, in 1970, Miss Mae concluded that it was time for her to return to Jamaica, this time permanently. Delton and Demetria would, therefore, remain in Britain. Before she left, she gathered her five children and grandchildren to take a group family photograph before they dispersed. The entire family were never again to reunite at the same time or live together in the same country.

Demetria felt shattered and demoralised. Life without Miss Mae changed everything. She returned to living with her mother and three younger brothers. Reluctantly she found herself having to build relationships afresh with a younger generation of siblings. Delton and her sister, Jumokah, had already left home. She was not close to her mother, and all her old anxieties returned. She vented her frustrations by being insolent and disrespectful to her mother and teachers at school, testing the limit of their patience. Her lackadaisical approach towards her education had a negative impact on her attitude and behaviour. It was the cause of her being suspended from school on two occasions. She had long since forgotten her father's counsel.

Amid this troubled period of her life, she revisited her unfulfilled promise to correspond with Mr Horton. In the early days, the communication between them was tentative and sporadic. But his timely intervention and words of encouragement, after yet another disagreement with her mother, served to uplift her spirits. In him, she had at least found an ally.

Mr Horton kindly explained to her, "With me, you can always express your opinions. I consider you adult, and while I may not agree with you, I respect you."

It was heartening for her to learn from Mr Horton that he was open to discussion. His affirmation that she had earned his respect meant a great deal to her. It would take each of them a while to establish their letter-writing, which before long served as a lifeline. They had to overcome the obvious frustration of experiencing long delays between every communication. He commented on this.

"Let nothing get you down and when in doubt tell your father even though it takes *infuriatingly* long for prompt letters to travel the five thousand miles. We need person to person TV communication via satellite. I hope it comes in my lifetime."

Favouring written communication with Demetria, Mr Horton never really benefited from TV satellite communication, even though the technology rapidly developed in his lifetime. Over the forthcoming years, their correspondence gained momentum, and at least on one occasion, Demetria did manage to surprise her father.

"Hi, sweetie," he wrote. "Blessings on you. You certainly have made up for being such a poor correspondent by writing a rather nice letter. Absurdly, I am already looking forward to the following one."

CHAPTER 11

Mr Horton intuitively wrote these timely and practical words to Demetria when she was facing difficult times at school. He was passionate about education, and he gave her something to think about.

"It is my considered view that the most important single word in any vocabulary is *try*. I cannot too strongly urge you to try with your training and never stop until you obtain meaningful qualifications. The training and experience you pursue today may well be saving your life and making your existence meaningful tomorrow."

He was right, of course, her application to learning could only be described as apathetic. This was conveyed in comments recorded in her school reports by most of her teachers. They were evidently trying harder than she was to gain satisfactory results from a more than capable student.

In another letter, he expressed his personal opinion on women and why he considered it important for them to be educated. Demetria had not long left school, and a year later, she had given birth to her first child. Mr Horton had again accurately evaluated the course her life was about to take.

"Make no mistake," he counselled, "women need educational

training and practical ability as much as a savings account, because the day may come when they find themselves faced with the prospect of being the sole provider for their household. Therefore, back to your English, even if you have to try a correspondence course."

In response to Mr Horton's suggestion, Demetria did make a concerted effort to enrol at college to study an A level in English. He continued relentlessly in his quest for her to get the best from her life, going as far as to reprimand her for her singular lack of interest in reading worthwhile literature. He felt that her reading material should at least include newspapers in order to keep abreast of local and international affairs. He admonished her.

"So you have taken umbrage to my true remark that if you can read but do not read, you are illiterate". He continued his point. "Interestingly, the same sun that melts butter hardens clay. I should have hoped that you would get my message and plan to increase your reading and to include newspapers in the material you do read."

She remained obstinate, not wishing to read newspapers which she felt held no interest for her. In the end, he conceded.

"I have, in fact, achieved only your reiteration that you still don't read newspapers. OK, so be it. I shall ultimately succeed. *You will read.* Learn well from the things happening around you."

In the end, he succeeded. Although Demetria learned little from the things happening around her, she did, in fact, become an avid reader.

Mr Horton's clear vision of how his children might attain their full potential as a way of bettering their lives was worded in his own unique way.

"If I have abused you and women generally by calling you unbecoming names, it is because I do not wish my women to be merely crackers in the bag. I should hope that some would at least be cream biscuits. How do you think I feel if someone says all the women in the Horton family are so-so crackers, not even one cream biscuit among them? So, I provoke you all to improvement. This also is a cause in which I ultimately will succeed. Under my savage training all of you — yes, even you, Demetria, — will be cream biscuits among crackers one day."

While Demetria eventually came to understand his desire to see his children attain success and realise their ambitions, to become as he termed it "cream biscuits", it was evident to her that he lacked the capacity to realistically support so many children living in multiple households in their endeavours, or to adequately contribute to their physical and emotional well-being. She even dared to question his ability to provide a credible role model. It was, therefore, down to the mothers of his children, who were all left by him as sole providers of their households, to raise his children and ensure that they achieved certain levels of success in their education and careers.

CHAPTER 12

By the mid 1970s, Mr Horton's welding business was struggling to make ends meet. The price of imported raw materials had rocketed. His shop had been robbed of equipment valued at over one hundred and fifty pounds, which was a considerable sum of money back then. He was forced to use borrowed tools to carry out his work. The running costs of his business would have to be re-evaluated. In the face of these problems, it was commendable that while remaining pragmatic, he still managed to stay resilient. He reasoned on his misfortune this way.

"However, I'm not allowing that to cause me to lose any sleep. But then, I have suffered loss caused by my own people, which I feel is worse than thieves, so it is no wonder the more I see of men, the more I love my dog."

The crippling effects of the economic downturn in Jamaica worsened throughout the 1970s and 80s, causing unprecedented hardship on the country as a whole, brought about from a significant borrowing agreement in 1978. Along with eight years of negative economic growth under the People's National Party (PNP), the state of the economy had been reduced to a mere shambles. This was not without its effect. The populace struggled to buy basic food items as the cost of living spiralled out of control.

Mr Horton admitted that he was left feeling he was in a "tail-spinning nose dive", none of which was helped by his mounting family responsibilities. At this juncture, his children numbered fourteen. The necessary constraints he had to apply to his finances made family life virtually impossible to enjoy.

In answer to Demetria's enquiry with regards to his wellbeing, in a somewhat fraught exchange between them, a frustrated Mr Horton commented on his feelings.

"Things are like trying to go upstairs on a downward escalator. You run vigourously only to remain in one place. Jamaica is in for a terrific time. The pressures here are near bursting point so every scrap of energy is used to keep alive."

CHAPTER 13

By now a grandfather but faced with the demands of his growing young family, he continued to be affected by the economic state of affairs, which rendered him unable to give his grandchildren anything at Christmas.

"Well, I missed you with Christmas wishes," he wrote to Demetria. "Sorry we haven't a thing to give, but God bless you. Dad"

He went on to explain why.

"Actually, I am coming to grips with inflation of the magnitude of over 100 percent on some items. Speaking on inflation, believe me, we are scraping the bottom of our meal barrel. But not to worry, as we are stubbornly fighting on determined to survive subversion, escalation, inflation—you name it.

It is not the stresses but our reaction to them that causes some to cope and some to yield in these times. I am afraid that Britain is so socially structured that too many are guaranteed food in the belly with which they become totally satisfied to the detriment of the building of their full personalities. Well one good thing that has come from this, reality has penetrated at last not from your letter alone, but we are now possessed of facts that make it clear that survival must come from sources provided by our Father in heaven".

"The position is bleak. Things are truly dim. Something will turn up," Demetria observed. Where from exactly? She failed to let him know.

Looking back at his fighting words, it was clear from her response that Demetria had misunderstood the true extent of the pressures he was up against. Mr Horton was struggling to keep his head above water. He was fighting from his corner for survival as if he was buried in the trenches of a war zone. His words, though, had struck a discordant note with Demetria. He saw people in Britain as being much better off than he was in Jamaica, leading him to describe Britain as being "so socially structured that food in the belly was guaranteed". He failed to appreciate the enormity of two issues in particular that widely affected the welfare of the black community in Britain—namely, living with racism and prejudice.

From the very outset of their arrival in Britain, the Caribbean community had faced overt racial discrimination. Far from feeling welcome, some, including Demetria, had been asked in the past by some white people, "Why don't you go back to your country?"

By 1968, black migration in Britain was seen as a threat to the best interest of the country. MP Enoch Powell strongly verbalised publicly what scores of people were thinking privately regarding the increase of black people migrating to Britain. His speech became known as "Rivers of Blood".[3] In it, he strongly criticised mass migration, specifically targeting Commonwealth immigration to Britain. He argued that the current level of immigration must be controlled.

If only Mr Horton had been privy to the daily challenges faced by the black community, perhaps he would have understood more clearly that no amount of food in the belly could nullify the effects of routinely being referred to as a "black nigger", "black wog", or a "black bastard". These cutting words were often expressed with venom and hatred against a race of people who wanted nothing more than to work to support their families and have access to decent housing. The social structure of the country had left many having to cope with unprecedented physical hardships in order to make ends meet. Black immigrants were accused of depriving white people of jobs and housing. Yet, it was indefensible that multi-housing, one of the few housing options available to blacks, could be described just a mere fifty years ago, as a "massive slum, full of multi-occupied houses, crawling with rats and rubbish".[4] Many found it hard to find fitting words to retaliate or convey their pain to their families back home. The mother country had failed them dismally. Their dissipated hopes and aspirations remained intangible.

As for Britain, it was far from being socially structured or well-ordered. The 1970s and 80s saw an explosion of suppressed black anger which was expressed through riots in all parts of the country. Second and third-generation blacks would be far less tolerant when confronted with racial discrimination. They were prepared to retaliate and speak out against the injustices their parent's had passively endured.

CHAPTER 14

Over the past few years, Demetria had observed from her travels to and from Jamaica that racism was not the sole domain of Britain. It existed in Jamaica too. A closer scrutiny of similar derogatory terms used by Jamaicans to describe skin colour and hair type—ranging from brown-skin gal, red neck, and coolie to pretty hair and picky nigger hair—revealed equally negative connotations. Neither do terms used to describe a mixed-race child—whose skin colour can lead to them being referred to as "neither fish nor fowl" or "half-caste"—hurt any less than the words used to describe a black person as a nigger or wog.

Racism had deftly carried its poison from generation to generation, and what an 85-year-old woman encountered when she was a girl growing up in colonial Jamaica bears testimony to the fact that skin colour was also an issue in the 1940s. A saying popularised in her time with regards to racial ethnicity was expressed in these words:

If you're white, you're inside.
If you're brown, hang around.
If you're black, step back.

Demetria had lacked the courage to speak out or explain to Mr Horton the effects of racism, or how it infringed on her daily life. Likewise, Mr Horton's misconstrued ideals on British society were outmoded. Their differing viewpoints had inadvertently led to what he described as a "gigantic misunderstanding". It had prevented them both from learning well from the things around them, or showing empathy when it was most needed.

CHAPTER 15

Mr Horton's letters establish a mere snapshot of his views on life. It was also true to say that despite not being the best role model, his vision and underlying intentions were well meant.

Was it an irrefutable paradox that all the women involved in Mr Horton's life were ultimately left by him vulnerable and "sole providers of their households"? Or did he merely reflect the values of a society, in which he happened to live, which had an estimated six out of ten single-parent households?

Demetria felt blessed that she had been able to look back on those letters and reconsider his words. In particular, a quote from an African proverb still resonated with her to this day. It had been instrumental in her maintaining positive relationships with her friends and family. Namely, "the same sun that melts butter hardens clay."

She learned from the saying that our reaction to a problem may cause us to stand on our pride and behave stubbornly, hardening our hearts like clay. On the contrary, if we yielded and became amenable to instituting needed changes to resolve negative circumstances, our action could be likened to melting butter. Resulting in a positive outcome.

Mr Horton woke up on 11 June; he was unwell, saying he felt he had a circulatory problem and feared he was having a stroke. He was admitted to hospital, where on the succeeding days, he remained in an unconscious or semi-conscious state from which he never recovered; nor was he ever really himself during that period. Paralysed on the right side, he was just 53 years old when his thoughts perished forever and his spirit departed from his body. He died on 16 June 1980.

Thankfully, Mr Horton was spared having to face the trauma of the unremitting hardships which worsened and continued to oppress the people months after his death. The nation, now in ugly mood, angrily turned the tide of fortune against the PNP. Prime Minister Michael Manley hastily held an ill-judged election in October 1980, despite having a full year's term of office still to run. It was one of the bloodiest in Jamaican history and was truly a case of "What gone bad a morning na come good a evening." A conservative estimate of 844 people were murdered; the true figures were probably much higher than reported. It was a crushing defeat for the PNP. The party had fallen dramatically out of favour with a nation of people who had once shown strong conviction in its leadership. Riding on the crest of a landslide victory, Edward Seaga, leader of the Jamaica Labour Party (JLP), was sworn in as Jamaica's fifth prime minister. Contrary to the hopes of the nation, Seaga was also unable to turn the economy around; it showed sporadic but unsustained growth — none of which helped much to alleviate the extreme economic pressures that encumbered the nation.

In one of his final letters to Demetria, Mr Horton affirmed his love for her in these comely words.

"Incidentally, I was absolutely thrilled with joy at your grace and wit in the delightful expression of your acceptance of my humble offer of love. What can I say to a child who says to me, 'If love is all you have to offer, then I accept it most gratefully, as I think it is one of the most wonderful things left in the world today'?

"Simply, thanks, sweetheart."

PART 2

SHORT STORIES
FOR NIGHT OWLS

MAS' WILLY—A
PIGGY'S TALE

In the 1930s Cecil Banham lived in the Blue Spring region of Belle Vue Tor, where he owned a number of properties. He was a kind pale-skinned man, whose own father was of Scottish descent. Despite being hard of hearing, he strongly disliked being shouted at by people due to his deafness. He preferred instead to be spoken to using a soft tone of voice. This was probably the main reason he got on so well with my uncle Morgan. He was always softly spoken and rarely ever known to raise his voice except under extreme provocation.

Cecil was enormously fond of animals, and nothing gave him greater pleasure than the pigs, goats, and chickens that he raised on his land. Every morning, his chickens would congregate around his ankles, squawking loudly as he scattered generous handfuls of corn on the ground. He also had some large mixed-breed dogs that he kept to guard the property. Tied up by day they welcomed the freedom from their chains to roam where they pleased at night, keeping any would-be intruders at bay. Panting deeply, they gazed intently at Cecil in the hope that he had brought them a treat. Today, they were not to be disappointed. He tossed six sizeable soup bones across to them. The dogs vied with each other, growling ominously to get possession of the largest bone. Their growls melted in the air when they realised there was nothing to fight about, Cecil had given them one bone each. He smiled indulgently as he watched their capers before moving on to see his goats. The goats rarely needed any treats at all. In truth, they would eat anything they could get hold of, including the washing on the line if he was not careful. He had a little word for each of them as he patted them gently on their heads. They snuggled lovingly into the circle of his arms.

Next, Cecil crossed the yard to his pigpen. He was busy planning a surprise for his grandson Morgan, who was due to visit him in the next few weeks. One of his large sows had recently given birth to a litter of eight lively piglets, five girls and three boys. He spent several minutes thoughtfully surveying their tiny wrinkled bodies as they nestled close to their mother to suckle greedily from her milk. His attention was particularly drawn to the largest boy. He was a spunky fellow who latched on to his mother's teat well ahead of the other piglets. His pale brown body was accentuated with dark brown patches. Cecil quietly observed him for several minutes; he was already showing signs of his curious character. Satisfied with his share of milk, he boldly left the safety of his mother to explore the strange and exciting smells he encountered around the yard. Just before one of his hens pecked him on the nose for getting too close to her chicks, Cecil bent down and scooped him up to restore him to his mother. He was satisfied this was the piglet that he wanted to give as a present to Morgan.

Ten-year-old Morgan could just about contain his excitement when his mother told him he would be visiting his grandfather

Cecil on Saturday. This would be a huge treat for him, as he would be allowed to travel there on his own. This was a big undertaking in those days, as it involved not only taking a bus but also the tram.

On Saturday morning, he was up at 6 a.m. He hurriedly showered and dressed, but it was only 6:15 a.m. by the time he had finished. No one else was up yet. He would have to wait for his mother to wake up and make his breakfast before he could begin his journey. He kept looking at the time, but the hands on the clock hardly seemed to move. At last, he could hear his mother stirring in the kitchen. She had his breakfast ready in no time, which he swiftly devoured. His mother handed him money for the bus and tram fare and a note for Cecil. He left the house to catch the bus. The best part of the journey was yet to come, which would be the tram to take him to Belle Vue Tor. He arrived in the nick of time at the busy terminal, as his tram was about to leave. It was packed to the rafters with people squeezed together like sardines in a can. Hangers-on were perched perilously on the tram's running board. Morgan wriggled his body through the tiniest gap to secure a space on the edge of a seat. The tram stuttered into life as it jerked forward. Morgan imagined he was being transported on a real train as the tram trundled along on the rails. He arrived at his destination, fervently wishing that his journey could go on forever.

Morgan walked in the warm sunshine for twenty minutes to get to his grandfather's home. He arrived in time for lunch. He washed his hands and face before taking a seat at the long mahogany dining table, where a large plate of rice and peas and brown stew chicken was placed in front of him. He eyed the plate hungrily. His mouth watered in anticipation. As an extra special treat, a tall glass of cold bright-red Sorrel, was set down on a coaster next to his plate. It had been brewed together with ginger from the first crop of the season grown in Cecil's garden before Christmas. As he slowly sipped the drink, he savoured the contrasting heat from the ginger and the coolness of the ice cubes that tinkled in the glass and mingled together to release a pleasant warm sensation that reached right to the back of this throat. A thin trickle of gravy ran down the side of his mouth from the chicken. Morgan was gently told off by his grandfather for using the back of his hand to wipe it away. He then allowed him to continue eating the remainder of his lunch.

He went on to enquire after the family as they sat comfortably together at the table. It was then Morgan remembered that he had not given him the note from his mother. He remedied his oversight straight away. Next, they shared a dish of freshly prepared pineapple as they talked together about their favourite topic, the trams. Cecil wanted to know how Morgan had fared on his journey. Morgan's eyes sparkled as he recounted the details. He told his grandfather how packed the tram had been, but it had not mattered at all, because he felt as if he were riding on a train. The cooling breeze that blew in from the open windows had transported him to another world. He listened patiently to his grandson's fantastical story. Cecil, who was himself knowledgeable about trams, explained to Morgan yet again that they had been in existence since November 1876, with electrification of the trams taking place much later, in 1897. Morgan had heard it repeatedly from his grandfather, but he never tired of hearing about his favourite form of transport. He drank the remains of the cool sorrel and leaned back in his seat, feeling contentedly full after the meal.

Later, they walked out together into the yard in the direction of the pigsty. Cecil told Morgan that he had something special that he would like him to see. His face lit up in sheer delight when he was told that he could choose a piglet to take home. He felt really important as he carefully studied each of the tiny piglets before deciding on the biggest one who squealed much louder than the rest of the litter and whose tiny bright eyes darted around mischievously. Cecil was elated that Morgan's choice had matched exactly his own. He carefully picked up the wriggling piglet and placed him in a cardboard box, which he tied up firmly with a stout piece of string and handed it across to Morgan. He cautioned him to be very careful with the box once he got on the tram.

After boarding the packed tram, the piglet's little snout pushed through one of the air holes on the side of the box as Morgan carefully balanced it on his knee. Luckily for him, he had been able to wedge himself tightly between two rather buxom Igla women. Their bright stiffly starched cotton gingham head scarves were tied neatly around their heads, and their voluminous blouses were held firmly in place secured by their large white aprons. They carried a huge basket each on their laps, crammed full with fresh ginger, scotch bonnet peppers, scallions, sweet potatoes, yams, okra, green bananas, and a range of spices, including pimento seeds, nutmeg, bay leaves, and cinnamon bark. The heady aroma from the spices lingered pleasantly in the air.

"Hey, Bwoy," one of the ladies called out loudly in a voice aimed at capturing the attention of fellow passengers. She cast her eye around to make sure they were listening before she continued.

"If you na mind sharp, me a go tek that pig with me to sell inna de market."

The whole tram erupted in loud, jovial laughter as the piglet let out a piercing squeal. It wriggled about restlessly in the box. Poor Morgan was mortified. His discomfiture knew no bounds. There was no time for him to indulge in his fantasy of travelling on a train. Every passenger on the tram turned their attention to him, fixing a prying eye on his piglet for the duration of his journey. He was most relieved when he reached his destination in Orange Street. He hung back nervously to let the Igla women get off ahead of him. He was afraid that they might change their minds and insist on taking his piglet to market with them. He paused for a moment under a large shady guango tree, protectively cradling the box. He continued watching their progress from a distance. He was amazed at the skill they showed balancing their huge loaded baskets on their heads. He continued his journey home, strolling at a leisurely pace across the main square to catch the bus. He felt the piglet squirming around in the box. He was glad that he did not have to carry it on his head like the Igla women. The rest of his journey was uneventful. He could not wait to get home to show off his prized piglet to everyone.

The novelty of having a piglet for a pet was embraced enthusiastically by the entire family. It rapidly blossomed into a really large, fat, and good-natured pet pig. He was a loving and entertaining addition to their household; he captivated the family's hearts. They affectionately named him Master Willy, or Mas' Willy for short. He had entire run of the yard, and with plenty of leftovers to eat each day, he contentedly rooted around stuffing himself to his heart's content, his large stomach was never empty. Much to the family's amusement, Mas' Willy kept Morgan's younger siblings and cousins constantly entertained by his non-stop pranks.

Mas' Willy became the talk of the neighbourhood, and although he was a "very important pig" (VIP) in his own home, regrettably, not everyone in the community felt the same way. Bitter complaints from disgruntled residents had been received regarding Mas' Willy by the local health authority. The family were found to be in breach of a law which stated that animals were not allowed to be kept in residential areas. They were duly served with an order to have Mas' Willy removed forthwith from the property.

"You are advised, from the date recorded in this letter, to get rid of your pig within the next thirty days," read Miss Amy to the assembled family.

She sucked hard on her teeth in disgust as she concluded reading the stern warning contained in the final paragraph of the letter. The news caused them all immense consternation. The younger members of the family were distraught; they regarded Mas' Willy as being their best friend. Others were moved to tears at the thought of losing him. Miss Amy was adamant she would devise a way to keep him. The thirty-day warning expired, and she ignored it. With nothing decided, Mas' Willy stayed happily in residence, completely ignorant of the family's quandary.

The problem was only taken seriously when a final warning and notification of a visit to inspect the property were issued to the family from the health authority. Sleepless nights and long hours of debate amongst them took place as they tried to work out Mas' Willy's best options. Should they give him away? Perish the idea.

Should they sell him? That too was unbearable. Surely, no harm would be done if they kept him in a pen instead of allowing him to roam freely around the yard. Nothing they had thought of so far would suffice. In the end, a plan was concocted which involved concealing Mas' Willy in one of the bedrooms on the day of the inspection—and keeping the inspector wholly distracted during the visit.

At last, the day of inspection arrived. Miss Amy, ably supported by the conspiring family, conducted the inspector around a lengthy tour of the yard and outside kitchen. An elongated discussion ensued on the fruit trees that were in season and which included those that were not. He was offered a loaded basket full of provisions from the garden, which he diplomatically declined. He was bemused, thinking to himself, *I wonder where dem hide dat Pig. Is this how dem plan to win me over, with a bribe? Dem stupid or what? Dem na know se di pig have fi go, and I am here to make dam sure it happen!*

With the inspection at last drawing to a close, the inspector was reassured that the pig, under no uncertain terms, had been removed from the premises. However, directly the family had escorted him as far as the gate, disaster struck. Much to their dismay, the distinct sound of Mas' Willy's loud squeals could be clearly heard coming from the direction of the house. It caused the inspector to hesitate in front of the gate. He turned and began slowly retracing his steps, following the sound. He stopped close to the veranda, where the sound of Mas' Willy's loud squeals gave the game away. A hugely embarrassed Miss Amy, backed up by the rest of the family, found herself frantically clutching at straws in a vain attempt to explain away the sound that had left the inspector in no doubt that the pig was still in residence. He was already mounting the steps. Standing on the veranda directly outside the bedroom door, he sternly demanded that it be opened immediately. Miss Amy gritted her teeth. Defeat stared her straight in the eye. She was left with no other choice but to open the door. Slowly turning the key in the lock, she reluctantly pushed it open. A greatly distressed Mas' Willy charged out of the bedroom, moving with such force, he was more like a raging bull than a pig. He charged around the veranda before almost knocking the inspector backwards down the steps as he bolted past him into the yard. The inspector's jaw dropped wide open in surprise when he saw Mas' Willy's substantial girth. Recovering his balance, he drew himself up to his fullest height to make the family feel very foolish. He looked them up and down disdainfully from head to toe in mock surprise.

A most indignant Mas' Willy had not been prepared to spend another second locked in the bedroom. He was equally angry and ravenous. His loud squealing and snorting continued for quite a while after he had been released. The inspector walked hurriedly to the gate to avoid making contact with Mas' Willy, who continued stomping around the yard like a spoiled brat, intent on showing the whole family the full extent of his displeasure. He was sore at being deprived of his normal root around the yard and devouring a large bowl of food for breakfast. Mas' Willy at last calmed down and trotted off to find his bowl of food. All was forgiven as, snorting loudly between huge mouthfuls of his favourite morsels, he contentedly demolished everything in his dish.

Pausing for a moment by the gate before leaving the premises, the health inspector turned to the family and uttered five definitive words that rang unpleasantly in everyone's ears.

"Get rid of that pig!"

Inevitably, the news spread round town like wildfire, much to the joy of certain residents. A local butcher seized the moment to personally call in to see Miss Amy. On sight of the generously proportioned pig, without delay, he offered to buy Mas' Willy at a price Miss Amy was unable to refuse. It was not quite the favourable solution to the problem the family had desired. They had to concede Mas' Willy's fate had now been irrevocably sealed. Oblivious to the fact that he was about to be terminated for good, he happily trotted off with the butcher.

That was how my uncle Morgan's pig sadly ended his most happy sojourn with our family. Mas' Willy, as you might expect, was turned into pork chops, sausages, bacon, and other tasty joints of meat.

THE JEWELLERY BOX

CHAPTER 1

Derek Forbes owned a jewellery shop in Petts Lane which he traded from Monday to Friday. He specialised in custom-made jewellery containing semi-precious gemstones. On Saturdays he ran a stall with his niece Rachel in Arabia Road Market where he sold less expensive and smaller items of jewellery. This lively market boasted a mixture of antique and salvage stalls making it ideal for customers who enjoyed a good rummage for one-off pieces. Business was brisk in the summer months, chiefly from visiting tourists as well as local residents. Rachel loved the social aspect of the job, especially when she could engage in light banter with her regular customers and other stall holders. Some customers returned week after week, in search of that special piece of jewellery to give as a birthday gift or just an unusual item to add to their collection. Others were mere opportunist; she had to keep her wits about her, for in a split second a small item of jewellery could quickly disappear into a pocket or handbag.

At 20 years of age, Rachel looked a good deal older. Her hair, which used to be thick, dark, and lustrous, was brittle and dry from neglect. It was drawn severely away from her face and tied neatly back in a ponytail. Deep lines creased her forehead, revealing the tell-tale signs of her anxious disposition. Derek called across to her from the other end of the stall.

"Fancy a cuppa and a bacon butty, Rachel?"

She nodded back in agreement. Until he had mentioned it, she had not realised how hungry she was.

"I will bring you one back" she replied.

Business had been slow today. The season was not yet in full swing; plus, it had rained all week. She welcomed a chance to take the short walk to a local cafe down the road. She knew the owner well and looked forward to having a natter and catching up on local gossip. On her way back to the stall, she glanced down a narrow side alley at a group of young men huddled around a silver Mercedes. The exchange of packets of drugs and money was made swiftly. Rachel kept her head low, hastily averting her eyes from the scene. The Mercedes sped past her, leaving in its wake circumstances reminiscent of her own life a few short months ago. Was this not the reason that she now worked on her uncle's stall?

CHAPTER 2

Rachel's parents had divorced when she was four years old. It was an acrimonious affair. Her parents had been unable to agree on anything. In due course, the family home was sold. Inflated house prices meant that neither parent had been in a position to buy another property outright. It was, therefore, a huge relief when Jessica Forbes, her grandmother, had stepped in to help out her eldest son Lawrence by offering Rachel a home. When she was old enough to choose where she wanted to live, her parents were in new relationships. Rachel expressed a firm desire to remain with her grandmother, to whom she had grown warmly attached. Jessica was strict but fair with her granddaughter. As far back as Rachel could remember, one of her grandmother's familiar maxims was "Bad company spoils useful habits." It had taught her to be cautious about her choice of friends.

How often had she heard those words from her grandmother, resonating in her ears? Lately, it had been her grandmother's appeal to her to stop and think, but Rachel had failed to heed the warning. The person leading her astray was Clifford, her boyfriend. He had meant everything in the world to her, but in the end, nothing at all.

CHAPTER 3

Rachel, Marcia, Jennifer, and Angela had been friends from primary school. The girls were inseparable. Marcia's round face was always full of smiles. Her effervescent personality infected them all. She had an endless stream of humorous stories and jokes to tell, and as a consequence, she was labelled the joker in the pack. Everything about Jennifer was long and thin, from her legs to her long, thin face. But her beautiful shoulder-length naturally blonde hair and compelling blue eyes were not easily overlooked. She was a popular, gentle, thoughtful girl with a most pleasing and amenable disposition. Angela was probably the most striking of the four girls. Her rich, shiny chestnut hair and show-stopping figure invariably turned heads whenever they were out together. Yet, of the four, she was the practical and conservative one. If ever there was a dispute between the girls, Angela had an uncanny way of resolving an issue in a way the other three could not. Who needed anyone else? At 16, they were top of their class, a force to be reckoned with. Until … well, how did it start?

Initially, the change was imperceptible. The girls normally met up after school, where they worked together on homework assignments. These were happy times, with the friendly rivalry that existed between them spurring them on to consistently achieve top grades. It was hard to believe that they had recently been in each other's company, for when they met up, they chatted endlessly, exchanging ideas on the latest fashion, boys, hairstyles, and makeup. They hung out together most weekends, either shopping, going to see movies, or just to have fun. Their primary focus and overall ambition to be a success and continue their studies at university never wavered, it kept them grounded.

Rachel met Clifford purely by chance; she stumbled as she bumped into him when she was hurrying home one evening from Jennifer's house. Jessica always worried if her granddaughter came home late. He was tall and dark, with refined features, dark brown eyes, and unusually long eyelashes for a man. His tight, curly black hair was fashionably cut, which gave him a suave elegance. This was complemented by his smart outfit. Their eyes locked for a split second as he firmly steadied her with his arm.

"Careful," he said. "What's the hurry?" His voice sounded soft and alluring.

Rachel's words came out in short, breathless bursts. "I'm late ... I-I must get home," she stammered.

She felt the pressure of his arm shift as he gently released her. She glanced up at his face. A thrill coursed through her body. *Wow, he's gorgeous*, she thought.

"I must go," she said as she stepped purposefully past him.

A chance meeting, or was it? In any case, that was how it all began.

CHAPTER 4

The next time Rachel saw Clifford, she was with the girls. They had been to the local shopping mall, and their bags were loaded. Their raucous laughter filled the air in response to another of Marcia's ace jokes. She noticed him sitting alone outside a cafe sipping a coffee whilst toying idly with his mobile phone. He fleetingly held her gaze as a knowing smile flickered across his mouth. She felt the heat in her body rising from her neck and flushing into her cheeks. Angela saw her reaction, but she said nothing. Rachel spun her head away self-consciously; she was quickly caught up again with the laughter of the girls.

At other times when Rachel was on her own, Clifford, would randomly appear, seemingly from nowhere, falling easily in step with her. It never occurred to her how familiar he was with her routine. Instead she was drawn to his welcoming smile which never failed to brighten her day. She was beguiled by his soft, deep voice, which had the quality of silk. On another occasion he made a point of properly introducing himself to her. His words flowed easily from his mouth, caressing her imagination.

He knew so much, she evidently had a good deal still to learn. Her walks home from school stretched late into the evening. A nearby canal became their favourite spot to wander along and chat together. She was taken in by his propensity to respond with empathy to problems that she was experiencing at school, or any conflicts she might be having with her grandmother. With few people around to distract them, Rachel's feelings for Clifford strengthened and, before long, she fell hopelessly in love with him.

"Where have you been?"

Jessica queried her rather sharply one evening when she arrived home late yet again.

"At Angela's," she replied defensively. Her cheeks flushed bright red. The lie did Angela no justice. She lived less than ten minutes' walk from Rachel's house. Yes it was true she had been at Angela's house, but when she left over two hours ago she discovered Clifford waiting for her on the corner. He had persuaded her to walk with him along the canal, an offer she had eagerly accepted. They meandered comfortably together hand-in-hand lost in deep conversation. She had lost track of time. Rachel strode defiantly past her grandmother to her bedroom slamming the door shut. Jessica let out a pained sigh; she was most displeased with Rachel's attitude. When it first started, she was willing to put it down to the rebellious stage most teenagers go through, testing the status quo, but lately, she was feeling distanced from her granddaughter. They had always enjoyed each other's company in the past. Part of her was reluctant to let go as her granddaughter was growing up and changing. She found it hard to accept that Rachel was a young woman with rights of her own. Nonetheless, she was prepared to try and maintain some common ground between them.

Rachel felt a pang of conscience, she was ashamed of her behaviour and its affect on her grandmother. She disliked that she was causing her pain. In unguarded moments, she had witnessed her sadness through the tears that welled up in her eyes when they had disagreements. Deep down she did truly love her, but under Clifford's influence he was starting to reshape her views. She became critical of her grandmother's good intentions which she now found suffocating. Furthermore, she loathed being treated like a child.

The tide really turned about six weeks after they began seeing each other. Clifford ramped up the pressure when he told Rachel in no uncertain terms one evening that he was quite fed up of meeting her in the street.

"How will I get to know you properly if all we ever do is walk along the canal and meet on street corners?" he argued petulantly.

His threat to terminate their friendship caused Rachel to feel obliged to comply. She was on the verge of embarking on an unfamiliar path of lies and deceit, which would eventually lead her into the dark side of Clifford's world.

CHAPTER 5

One Saturday evening, Clifford invited Rachel to see a movie. She was over the moon until she started thinking through the logistics. What would she tell her grandmother and the girls? To appease her grandmother, she decided to use the girls as the obvious scapegoat. Happily for her the strategy worked.

Dressing carefully for the occasion, Rachel paid close attention to her hair and make-up. The result was pleasing. She accessorised her outfit choice of a teasingly suggestive pale blue low-cut top and skinny-fit jeans with a dazzling matching necklace, earrings, and bracelet set. Her grandmother reminded her to be home by no later than 10:30 p.m.

"Yes, of course, Grandma," she replied as she skipped happily out of the front door.

"You look nice," Clifford commented as he ran his eyes slowly and seductively up and down her perfectly formed body. Her freshly washed hair glistened as it caught the rays of light. Her jewellery suddenly attracted his attention. He leaned across her to make a closer inspection of her necklace and bracelet. Letting out a long whistle he asked her, "Where did you get these from? They must have cost a pretty penny" he observed.

Rachel could not have wished for a better response. She

proudly informed him of their family tradition that each year on her birthday, her uncle Derek would present her with a fine piece of jewellery. Over the years, she went on to explain to him, these had amassed into an impressive collection. Clifford carefully digested the information.

They sat closely together at the back of the cinema. The darkness encircling them like a soft velvet blanket. The luminosity of the screen cast long shadows down his face, defining the sharpness of his nose and the softness of his mouth. He slipped his arm around her shoulders. She thrilled to his touch.

"Are you OK?" he whispered gently into her ear.

She felt her heart rate accelerate as he pulled her towards him. She nestled her head comfortably against his shoulder. He leaned closer, his face brushed lightly against her cheek. He sought her lips, from which he drank thirstily in an extended kiss. Rachel flushed with unrestrained pleasure. It was the first date where Clifford had presumed such familiarity with her. She struggled to remember the name of the film they had just seen. She was floating on air when they left the cinema.

The weeks that followed left Rachel feeling as if she was permanently on a rollercoaster ride. Thoughts of Clifford filled her every waking hour.

"Rachel, is there anything wrong? You seem a bit distracted," Marcia enquired.

She snapped out of her latest reverie and replied, "No, nothing at all. I am a little tired—that's all.

She forced a weak and unconvincing smile as she tried to keep up with the flow of conversation. Marcia, Jennifer, and Angela exchanged fleeting glances between them and shrugged their shoulders in disbelief.

It was not long before Rachel's excuses to her grandmother and the girls escalated into brazen lies. She masterfully invented new ones each day. Her neighbour needed her to babysit. She was helping her grandmother to sort out her wardrobe. It was her turn to cook dinner. She had promised to blow-dry Angela's hair. On and on it went. No wonder she felt tired. Even her attendance at the after-school study sessions, formerly such a pleasurable activity, became infrequent. Alarm bells triggered the girls' curiosity.

Her grandmother's querulous voice of disapproval seemed to continually warn her about her "bad associations". She ignored her inner instinct and threw caution to the wind. Not wishing to incur Clifford's displeasure she sacrificed her friendship with the girls' in exchange for the intimacy of his company.

Clifford lived alone in a fresh modern two-bedroom apartment close to the centre of town. Clever use of colour and contrasting textures throughout the space gave it the atmosphere of a tranquil sanctuary. Rachel enjoyed relaxing there. She was unmindful of Clifford's dark side or his late-night activities which occurred after she had left his home.

Angela and Jessica began probing into her affairs. They wanted to know where she was spending her evenings. Jessica was also investigating Rachel's whereabouts. To that end she had telephoned Angela to check up on Rachel only to discover she was not there. Neither had she been at school that day—nor, she learned from Angela, on quite a few other days. Her attendance had worryingly dropped to roughly two days a week. Jessica was shocked.

"How could that be?" she asked Rachel's teacher before proceeding to berate her angrily for ten minutes on the phone defending Rachel. To the best of her knowledge, she explained to her teacher, she left home every day for school at the same time. If she was not at school, then where was she going? The school was unable to enlighten Jessica any further on the subject, and the conversation was coldly terminated on that note. Angela, who until then had kept quiet, felt it was time to approach Rachel face-to-face to confront her regarding the matter. She was unprepared for the encounter. Throughout their years of friendship, they had never ever quarrelled. Yet today, their row had been ferocious. Rachel let rip at Angela with a string of vicious and hurtful words. Angela was shaken to the core. Rachel also, much to her chagrin, did not recognise herself either after such an unreasonable outburst.

Later, when she arrived home, the second she put her key in the front door, her grandmother pounced on her demanding an explanation. Still highly strung from her argument with Angela, to her greater shame, she turned aggressively on Jessica screaming at her to leave her alone. Shaking with rage, she slammed the door to her bedroom. Another of her grandmother's sayings came into her mind. "Oh, what a tangled web you weave when first you practice to deceive." She felt like a tightrope walker, one false move and she would slip from the high wire. Her jagged nerves were on edge. All she wanted to do was get away from everyone. She put on her coat and left the house.

When she arrived at Clifford's flat, she let out a low sigh as she flopped down onto the sofa. Clifford, sensing her stress and being attentive as ever, spoke soothingly to her. This was what Rachel loved about him best; he never failed to understand what she was going through.

"This will help you to relax," he said gently as he handed her a tiny white pill and a glass of water "It's designed to take your troubles away" he told her. It was as simple as that.

He was right. Within a few minutes, the cares of the outside world were blotted out. Being in his company was what she cared about most. She forgot about her row with Angela or her grandmother worrying about her returning home late. She stayed the night and left early in the morning. How could she possibly have known where those pills were about to take her?

CHAPTER 6

Her avariciousness for the pills rapidly escalated. Even though they reduced her stress levels, they obscured their insidious infiltration into her body, which led to her requiring significantly higher doses to achieve the same effect. Clifford was extremely obliging; he supplied her with all she could consume.

She was confronted again about him. This time, Marcia and Jennifer were in the driving seat. She felt like a trapped fox being smoked out of its den. How dare they question her about him? In a heated exchange, they forced her to see things about him she had not wanted to believe.

"What does he do for work?" Marcia queried Rachel.

"You have no idea, do you?" Jennifer challenged her.

They were right. Of course, she did not have a clue. He had never given her any reason to doubt his intentions until now.

Rachel countered back. "What business is it of yours? He has everything he needs. You've seen him. He's always well dressed, and money is never a problem for him."

"You do know he is seeing other women," Jennifer retorted sharply.

Rachel obstinately covered for him. "That's utter nonsense. Where would he get the time? He spends every waking hour with me" she lied. "You are just jealous," she responded smugly. Walking away from the girls, she then turned round to scream at them. "Leave me alone."

Rachel could not wait to get over to Clifford's house to collect her pills. Boy, was she in need of them today. When she arrived at his flat, flushed and agitated, not only did he refuse to give them to her, he had the audacity to inform her that the pills were no longer free. Shaken and taken aback; she hardly recognised the callous tone of his voice. His behaviour was alien to her. She was bewildered and at a loss to understand what was happening. Why had things changed? She stubbornly reasoned that he had always given them to her whenever she needed them. She stared meekly up at him in sheer disbelief. She pleaded with him to let her have a few pills. She assured him she would get the money to pay for them in the future if that was what he wanted.

"Oh, yes," he snarled at her. "You will certainly pay for them from now on."

"How much are they?" she asked him guilelessly.

When he told her the price, she was stunned. She had no idea where she was going to raise that kind of money. Jessica and uncle Derek had always given her a generous monthly allowance, which she spent lavishly on her clothes, hair, and makeup. Out of it she had managed to save around one thousand pounds towards her summer holiday to Cyprus. The girls had planned to go when they had finished their exams. She possessed no other income.

She went to the bank and withdrew four hundred pounds, thinking that would be sufficient to resolve the problem, and for a couple of weeks, it seemed everything was back to normal. That was until more money was needed. This time, she emptied her account against the advice of the bank clerk. The pills were her number one priority; she was finding it near impossible to get through even a day without them.

Clifford was well aware that she was struggling to find money to pay for the pills.

"Why don't you pawn some of that fancy jewellery you have?" he suggested derisively.

Rachel had no idea of the value of her jewellery. She started selecting random pieces from her jewellery box every few weeks, taking them to a local pawnbroker. She gave little thought to the care and pride with which her uncle Derek had taken to choose each piece of jewellery he had given her. She knew only that it provided the money to pay for this monstrously growing habit.

She gave up trying to attend school and avoided the girls if she ever bumped into them in the street. She was now all too familiar with their views of Clifford. Furthermore, she was in too deep to admit that they had been right about him.

Her reflection in the mirror terrified her. Her clothes hung loosely from her shrunken and emaciated body. Her once beautiful hair was dry and unkempt. She rarely had time to wash properly let alone put on makeup. She hung around Clifford's house like a bad smell. He persistently verbally abused her, tearing her self-esteem and confidence to ribbons.

Poor Jessica was beside herself. Rachel's teacher had urgently contacted her again to express her unease regarding Rachel's dramatic weight loss and non-attendance at school. Jessica's stubborn conviction caused her to still unfairly blame the girls. "Bad Company" she indignantly and unjustly called them. It was distressing for her to see Rachel sinking lower and lower before her very eyes. They rowed often and bitterly. Deep down, she struggled with herself to admit it was Rachel who was the problem. How much longer could she continue in denial?

Now in pressing need of more pills, locked in her room, Rachel battled with her shaking, clammy fingers to open the clasp on her jewellery box. At last it yielded. She stared into the box dumbfounded. All that was left of her treasured jewellery was a large platinum and diamond pendant she had been given by her uncle when she turned 13 years old. It was her most cherished piece. What should she do? She was frantic. The pendant would definitely fetch a lot of money. It should keep her going for a few more weeks, she reasoned. With the greatest of reluctance, she mused over the idea of pawning it. Then she remembered that her grandmother kept a sizeable sum of cash at home for emergencies. Such was the trust that formerly existed between them. Her grandmother was out shopping, and Rachel knew exactly where to find the money. For the first time in her life, she stole £300 from her grandmother. Completely overwhelmed by the sheer enormity of her action, Rachel had to admit that her life was running out of control, and it was most unfortunate that it was far beyond her power to help herself to get back on track.

CHAPTER 7

By the time Clifford opened the door to her on the third ring of his doorbell, Rachel was in a state of high agitation. Her body felt hot, yet her hands were drenched in cold sweat. She shivered uncontrollably as the cool evening air chilled her to the bone. She pulled the belt of her coat tighter and turned up the collar. She failed to understand why he had not invited her in. She was feeling cold and needed to get into the warmth. Instead, he blocked the doorway, preventing her from entering his flat.

"Have you got the money?" he growled at her in a harsh cold voice she was rapidly becoming accustomed to him addressing her with.

In fact, she could not recall the last time he had said anything nice to her other than take money from her. Today was no exception. She also suspected that he was seeing another woman, but she didn't dare to ask him fearing the consequences. She blamed herself for neglecting her personal care, convincing herself that was where the problem lay. Before she left home, she had attempted to apply some makeup and freshen up her hair. Her smudged and blotchy foundation and randomly smeared lipstick was a stark reminder of how chaotic her life had become. She craved interminably for the affection and attention he used to show her when they had first met.

"Aren't you going to ask me in?" she asked him coyly.

"No, I have visitors. Where is the money?" he repeated bluntly.

She trembled involuntarily as she handed him the money. He grabbed it roughly from her hand to count it before pushing a folded packet of pills in her direction. Reaching for them, she examined the packet before stuffing them into her handbag.

"Is that all?" she ventured to ask him in a surprised tone. She could have sworn that last week, the same amount of money bought twice the amount of pills.

"What do you expect?" he spat the words at her. She winced as if she had been physically hit in the face. "Anyway," he continued in a rough voice, "as I said before, I've got visitors. I must go!"

He slammed the door harshly in her face. An icy cold feeling of desperation welled up inside her. Burning tears of shame ran down her cheeks as she ran towards the canal, feeling hurt and confused. Clifford had torn her whole world apart. She wandered aimlessly along the canal, frantically trying to piece together the remaining fragments of her life. The recollection of her and Clifford strolling hand-in-hand along the canal they had once loved so dearly had lost its charm and was but a distant memory. Today, the water looked unappealing, with its dark and dingy surface smothered in thick pea-green duck weed. She popped two pills in her mouth, swallowing them with difficulty. She shuddered hopelessly. It would take another four pills before she began to relax.

Rachel was too embarrassed to contact the girls; she had shut them out of her life for months. Yes, the weeks had turned into months. Her grandmother had told her that they had all been accepted into the universities of their choice. She was happy for them, but it was paradoxically a bitter pill to swallow.

Her eighteenth birthday was a few days away. She had imagined that she would at last bring Clifford over to meet her grandmother and uncle Derek. Instead, now excluded from his life, she perversely depended on him now more than ever.

She shrugged her shoulders in an effort to move forward.

"What the heck?" she said. "I have enough pills to get me through a few more days."

She walked slowly home. Turning the key in the lock and pushing open the door, she was startled to find uncle Derek waiting for her in the corridor.

CHAPTER 8

In the end, Jessica had no choice but to muster up the courage to confide in her son. He also understood from his mother how rapidly things had declined, creating an unpleasant atmosphere between herself and Rachel. The issue came to a head when she realised that Rachel had stolen her money. It was impossible to deny that there was something amiss. Phone calls to Marcia, Angela, and Jennifer revealed they were equally concerned about Rachel's obvious decline. She was wounded to the core of her heart to learn from the girls that her granddaughter was under the influence of a local pimp and drug dealer. Clifford was known in the area. He was to be blamed for ruining the lives of more than a few vulnerable girls by getting them hooked on drugs.

A local pawnbroker had been in contact with Derek. He had brought his attention to the fact that his niece had recently pawned a number of valuable pieces of jewellery at his shop. Fortunately, for Derek he was able to redeem all the jewellery. Next, he paid Clifford a visit. Watching from across the street, having followed Rachel to his house, he had witnessed her having the door slammed shut in her face. He could see from her appearance how distressed and upset she was. It aggravated him to see her being humiliated in this way.

Clifford was visibly surprised to receive a visit from Derek. The two men squared up to each other like two battling deer with their horns locked. Derek delivered a severe warning to Clifford to leave his niece alone. It was an unpleasant encounter. He was a nasty piece of work, but Derek stood his ground, firmly refusing to be intimidated.

Later that evening, he had a heart to heart with Rachel. This was the first time in a very long time they had spent any quality time together.

"Come on, Rachel," he pleaded with her. "Your grandmother and I love you, whatever happens. We are not here to judge you."

His words broke her spirit; she had never in her life felt so lost and unhappy as she did now. Her eyes filled with tears of anguish. She hated them seeing her like this. Yet she was relieved. This was the wake-up call she needed.

CHAPTER 9

Marcia, Jennifer, Angela, her uncle Derek, and her grandmother have all continued supporting Rachel. With their thoughtful and loving care, she has gradually begun the long process of withdrawing from the harmful drugs that were ruining her life.

For additional support to manage her addiction, Rachel had taken the initiative of joining a drama group that worked with recovering addicts. At first she found it daunting to explore her personal issues with eight other participants through the use of role-play and drama. As the group bonded, she realised that they were all vulnerable, but by working together they could become stronger in their resolve to successfully conquer their addictions.

Derek offered Rachel a Saturday job on his market jewellery stall, in addition to helping him out mid week in his shop during busy periods. As her knowledge of gems increased, so did her self-belief. She demonstrated to her uncle that she wanted to be involved in all aspects of his business. He encouraged her to sign up to study gemmology at her local college. Rachel gratefully accepted his offer to pay her college fees. Her life was beginning to feel structured and purposeful, and she was determined not to waste this valuable chance. She had a lot to prove to herself as well as her grandmother and the girls.

As for Clifford, his next victim turned out to be a pretty young female police officer working undercover from the vice squad. She made short work of having him arrested for pimping and possession of class A and B drugs. He was currently serving a seven-year jail sentence.

The girls had planned a reunion at the weekend. Rachel could hardly believe that she had not been out with them for over four years. She felt apprehensive as she carefully dressed for the occasion. She knew it would be good for her self-confidence to be with her true and loyal friends. For that reason, she decided to wear the only piece of jewellery that she had not pawned, her platinum and diamond pendant. She contemplated the qualities attributed to platinum and diamonds. Platinum, was known for its strength and durability, while characteristically, every diamond was unique; its size, colour, and cut established its true value.

When she was given the pendant at thirteen years of age, it had marked the start of her journey to womanhood. Now it signified the start of a much brighter and happier future for Rachel. Tonight was not about anyone's success or failure. She knew it was going to take all her strength and determination to be strong and allow her true value to shine just like the remarkable qualities of platinum and diamond. She took in a deep breath before she pulled open the front door.

THE KEY TO THE MATTER

Jerry walked slowly through St James's Park. It was an unusually warm summer evening early in July. The final traces of the earlier brilliant evening sunset were still visible. His face was damp with perspiration which he wiped dry with a large clean white handkerchief. He stretched and yawned and stuffed it back into his trouser pocket. Continuing his walk out of the park, he crossed the road into Birdcage Walk before turning right into Storey's Gate. He heard Big Ben chiming loudly nine times. The noise from the bell resounded intrusively shattering the peacefulness of the evening. He smiled, inwardly thinking, *What would we do without Big Ben to keep track of time?*

He was exhausted. He yawned again as he arrived at his front door in Queen Anne's Gate. He pushed his key into the lock, slammed the door shut, walked past his cat into the living room, and threw himself on the sofa. The cat meowed loudly in disgust; he was hungry. Jerry was already snoring loudly.

On the street outside, a shadowy figure could be seen approaching the front door which Jerry had gone through earlier. It was illuminated by a street lamp that highlighted the key sticking out of the lock. The person, a smartly dressed medium-built man wearing a thin grey flannel suit, looked surreptitiously over his shoulder and then up and down the street to make sure that no one else was about. Satisfied the street was all clear, he crept stealthily towards the door and slowly mounted the steps. He made a swift examination of the key and then he pressed his ear closely to the door. He could hear no sound coming from within. Before he could stop himself, he had already turned the key which rotated easily in the lock. The heavy door swung silently open. Carefully removing the key, the man slipped it into his pocket.

His heart pounded in his chest as he lingered in the doorway. Still hesitating, he shot another furtive glance over his shoulder before he carefully closed the door and proceeded to creep forward cautiously into the hallway.

The sound of someone snoring grew louder as he gradually inched his way towards a partially open door at the end of the corridor. A thin ray of pale yellow light spilled from the room just ahead of him.

Suddenly, without any warning, a large ginger cat shot past him, his loud *meow* pierced the air, startling him. He stumbled and lost his footing. Blindly reaching out he grabbed hold of a table to steady himself. He heard a noisy crash as he knocked over a vase of flowers from the table. At the same time, his feet inadvertently gave way from underneath him, and as he lost control of his footing he slid in the spilled water from the flowers to land with a heavy thud hitting his head with a bone-crunching crack on the smooth polished marble tiled floor.

"Who's that?" yelled a cross-sounding voice from within the room.

The man on the floor was too dazed to reply. He reached up

to rub his sore head, while at the same time attempting, with the greatest difficulty to get back onto his feet. He felt panic striken, unable to move, he listened to the sound of heavy footsteps coming urgently towards him. His arms flayed helplessly around like a bird with a broken wing. He desperately searched around him to find something to hold on to raise himself off the floor. It was too late he had been caught. A large figure hovered over him.

"Who's that?" the angry voice again yelled, this time even louder.

The man on the floor was blinded for a split second by a bright beam of light from a torch being shone directly onto his face. At the same time, the cat landed on his chest, causing him to tumble backwards. Laying prostrate on the floor, James found himself looking directly into the face of his twin brother, Jerry. Both men were momentarily stunned, but their faces relaxed into wide grins as recognition dawned. Jerry let out a deep, throaty chuckle and reached out to help James up onto his feet. James followed suit, and soon the brothers were falling about in uncontrolled mirth.

It emerged that James had forgotten his key at work, whilst Jerry had left his key in the front door. James had suspected something was amiss when he saw the key in the door. He immediately thought there might be an intruder in the house, hence the reason for his cautious entry. Jerry also suspected that he had come across a burglar who was up to no good. They continued laughing together in sheer relief. The disgruntled cat again meowed loudly, he was still waiting to be fed.

These likeminded brothers had to agree that all was well that ended well, and that was the key to the matter!

SOURCES

1. Nurses and TB in 1950. Holme, Chris (2016)
2. Breathing exercises for asthma. Thomas, Mike & Bruton, Anne (2014) Breathe. 10 312-322.10.1183/20734735.008414
3. Enoch Powell – 'Rivers of Blood' Speech to Conservative Association (1968) https://www.britpolitics.co.uk/british-politics-speeches-enoch-powell-rivers-of-blood/
4. History of Notting Hill - The Guide to Notting Hill https://www.thehill.co.uk/index.php/about-notting-hill/history-of-notting-hill/

Lightning Source UK Ltd.
Milton Keynes UK
UKHW020632241020
372154UK00006B/236